THROUGH A MIRROR DARKLY

I leafed through the artist's pad and came to a self-portrait. Michelle Thayer in Michelle Thayer's hand. It was the picture of a girl on the very cusp of womanhood. A girl full of the energy of that moment. Smiling brightly—beaming even— her cheeks high, her eyes bright.

I glanced up at Mrs. Thayer. She was nodding at me. This—this self-portrait—was what she had wanted me to see.

"Look at it, Mr. Wells," she said. "She drew that a week before she died. Look at it good. That's not the face of a girl who killed herself."

Again I looked up at her.

"My daughter was murdered."

INTRODUCING

JOHN WELLS,
ACE CRIME REPORTER,
THE NEW YORK STAR.

Bantam Books offers the finest in classic and modern American murder mysteries. Ask your bookseller for the books you have missed.

Stuart Palmer
THE PENGUIN POOL MURDER
THE PUZZLE OF THE HAPPY
  HOOLIGAN
THE PUZZLE OF THE RED
  STALLION
THE PUZZLE OF THE SILVER
  PERSIAN

Craig Rice
THE LUCKY STIFF

Rex Stout
BROKEN VASE
DEATH OF A DUDE
DEATH TIMES THREE
FER-DE-LANCE
THE FINAL DEDUCTION
GAMBIT
THE RUBBER BAND

Max Allan Collins
THE DARK CITY

William Kienzle
THE ROSARY MURDERS

Joseph Louis
MADELAINE
STEPHANIE

M. J. Adamson
NOT TIL A HOT JANUARY
A FEBRUARY FACE
REMEMBER MARCH

Conrad Haynes
BISHOP'S GAMBIT, DECLINED

Barbara Paul
FIRST GRAVEDIGGER
THE FOURTH WALL
KILL FEE
THE RENEWABLE VIRGIN
BUT HE WAS ALREADY DEAD
  WHEN I GOT THERE

P. M. Carlson
MURDER UNRENOVATED

Robert Crais
THE MONKEY'S RAINCOAT

Ross Macdonald
THE GOODBYE LOOK
SLEEPING BEAUTY
THE NAME IS ARCHER
THE DROWNING POOL
THE UNDERGROUND MAN

Margaret Maron
THE RIGHT JACK

William Murray
WHEN THE FAT MAN SINGS

Keith Peterson
THE TRAPDOOR

Robert Goldsborough
MURDER IN E MINOR
DEATH ON DEADLINE

Sue Grafton
"A" IS FOR ALIBI
"B" IS FOR BURGLAR
"C" IS FOR CORPSE

R. D. Brown
HAZZARD
VILLA HEAD

A. E. Maxwell
JUST ANOTHER DAY IN PARADISE
THE FROG AND THE SCORPION

Rob Kantner
BACK-DOOR MAN
THE HARDER THEY HIT

Joseph Telushkin
THE UNORTHODOX MURDER OF
  RABBI WAHL

Richard Hilary
SNAKE IN THE GRASSES
PIECES OF CREAM

Carolyn G. Hart
DESIGN FOR MURDER
DEATH ON DEMAND

Lia Matera
WHERE LAWYERS FEAR TO TREAD
A RADICAL DEPARTURE

THE

TRAP DOOR

KEITH PETERSON

BANTAM BOOKS
TORONTO • NEW YORK • LONDON • SYDNEY • AUCKLAND

This novel is a work of fiction. Names, characters, places, and incidents are either the product of the author's imagination or are used fictitiously. Any resemblance to actual events or locales or persons, living or dead, is entirely coincidental.

THE TRAPDOOR

A Bantam Book / March 1988

ISBN 0-553-27073-7

Published simultaneously in the United States and Canada

Bantam Books are published by Bantam Books, a division of Bantam Doubleday Dell Publishing Group, Inc. Its trademark, consisting of the words "Bantam Books" and the portrayal of a rooster, is Registered in U. S. Patent and Trademark Office and in other countries. Marca Registrada. Bantam Books, 666 Fifth Avenue, New York, New York 10103.

PRINTED IN THE UNITED STATES OF AMERICA

O 0 9 8 7 6 5 4 3 2 1

This book is dedicated to the Samaritans of New York,
who stand between the despairing and the darkness.

PROLOGUE

Janet Thayer told it this way.

She was a little the worse for drink when she came home that night. It was getting to be a habit with her. A bad habit. She'd taken to keeping a pint of gin in the storeroom behind the syringes. She'd sneak in there now and then for a quick snort. That, and a beer or two with dinner, killed the pain. And by the time she came home, she was high and happy. She was, as she put it, "feeling okay."

When she came in the door of her house, it was after midnight. That was the shift she'd pulled this month, the late shift. She dumped her jacket on the floor and went to the kitchen. She was still wearing her nurse's uniform, still dressed in white. She went to the fridge, pulled out a beer, cracked it open, knocked it back. She lit a cigarette, too, and tossed the match in the sink. She had her fingers wrapped around the neck of the beer bottle, the cigarette jutting out between her knuckles when she went upstairs to her daughter's room.

She opened the door a little and peeked in. She puckered her lips and blew a kiss at the bed. She'd almost pulled the door shut, when she paused and peeked in again.

The bed was empty.

She was afraid right away—that's the way she told it. She was afraid from the very first moment, as if she knew. She turned on the light of the little room and stared at the empty bed. The smoke drifted up between her fingers, and the beer was cold in her hand, and she was afraid.

She left the room. She hurried down the stairs.

Her first thought was to call the police, but she didn't. Her second was to call her daughter's friends. She didn't do that either. She walked outside instead.

2

She stood on her own doorstep with her arms crossed and shivered. There was a fierce wind blowing, and she felt a chill all through her. She was plenty sober now.

The house was surrounded by forest. The leaves were still flush and colorful on the trees. They rattled and whispered all around her. The moon was full. She could see the branches swaying in the silver light. She dropped her cigarette, crushed it with her shoe, and set the beer bottle down. She stepped away from the door and walked around to the back of the house.

She walked into the woods. Maybe her daughter had gone for a walk. Maybe it was just that. She followed a thin, overgrown dirt path through the trees. She kept her arms crossed on her chest, moved her eyes back and forth, looking. She was about fifty yards into the forest when she stopped short.

It was the voice of a tree close by her that stopped her. The voice of one of its branches bending in the wind. Its voice was different from the others. Louder, more mournful. This branch was carrying an extra burden. This branch had a dirge to sing.

Janet Thayer turned and saw her daughter. She saw her daughter's silhouette against the white moon. She saw her daughter's figure dangling in the air above her, held there by a rope tied around a branch. The girl's dead figure twisted to the right. Paused. Twisted to the left again.

That was all Janet Thayer could tell. That was all she remembered.

1

It happened less than two months later, on a Friday. I was telling stories to Lansing and McKay when Robert Cambridge, the managing editor of the *New York Star*, walked into the city room. Cambridge likes Lansing because she has long straight blond hair that shines like silk and because she has a long body that rises and falls like a sigh and because she is beautiful. Cambridge likes McKay because McKay doesn't put in for overtime. I, on the other hand, am not beautiful and I put in for every second. Cambridge doesn't like me. Lansing and McKay like me. Cambridge doesn't like that.

Lansing and McKay had found me asleep in my cubicle that morning. Lansing grabbed my shoulder and gave me a shake. I unburied my head from my arms.

"Ow," I said.

"Morning, Wells," said Lansing. McKay was standing behind her, laughing. "It's eight-thirty, baby. The happy bustle of the city room is swirling around you. Rise and shine."

"Oh man," I said. My head was throbbing. My eyes felt like they'd been dabbed at the corners with epoxy. There was some of the stuff on my tongue too. My spine—my rapidly aging spine—had shrunk in the night. "Oh man, oh man," I said.

Lansing laughed a little. She had rich lips, and the way they curved when she laughed would've made a living man breathless. Her oval face was smooth, her high cheeks pink. She was wearing white slacks and a light green blouse that showed off the long terrain of her. "I'll get you some coffee," she said. I watched her walk to the machine on the table by the wall.

"Whatcha got?" said McKay.

I turned to him, tried to prop my eyes open a little wider. For a moment I couldn't remember what I had. "Uh . . . oh, I got the guy . . . the secret witness . . . in the Dellacroce trial."

McKay has the sort of face you expect to find on a jar of strained squash: round, bare, innocent. Now it was his eyes that widened. "You got his name?"

"Yeah, everything. Isn't the paper out yet? Should be page one."

"You hog page one again?" said Lansing. She put a Styrofoam cup on my desk. The coffee was black and steaming.

I rubbed my shoulder. "Don't you guys read this paper?"

"Nah," said Lansing. "We know it stinks, we write it."

"Wells got the witness against Dellacroce," McKay said.

"Oooh, nice. You I.D. him?"

"Nah. If I I.D. him, he might trip and fall into a meat-grinder." I rubbed the stubble on my face, yawned. "I'd rather wait and let him nail Dellacroce. I have this prejudice against people nicknamed Stiletto."

"So why were you here all night again? Drink your coffee," Lansing said.

I reached for my coffee. A pain shot through my shoulder. I flinched.

"What is it?" said Lansing.

"Nothing."

"It's your shoulder. Damn it, I wish you'd go home and sleep sometimes."

"I traded," I said. I grabbed the cup with my other hand. Sipped it. "I told Cicelli I had the name, and traded for an indictment." Lansing smiled and shook her head. "Don't look at me like that, Lansing," I said.

"Who'd you get?" said McKay.

At which moment Alex, the copyboy, walked by. He tossed the morning edition onto my lap. "Nice going, Pops," he said.

The paper lay open on my knees. The banner said: TRANSIT
CHIEF INDICTMENT SOUGHT.

"Wow," said McKay.

"Did he call me Pops?" I said.

"Nice going, sweetie. You are something," said Lansing.

"That little pinprick called me Pops."

McKay took the paper, a tabloid. He opened it to page
three, leaned against the desk in the cubicle across from me
and read the story. "Oh," he said. "Oh, nice. Nice, nice,
nice, Wells." Lansing leaned next to him, looking over his
shoulder.

"Thanks." I took out a cigarette, lit it. Leaned back
against my desk, facing them.

"Look at this. I never get stuff like this," McKay said.
McKay was our staff poet. The guy you send out to write the
kid-with-cancer story. The one who can take a sidebar on a
fire victim and make you cry. He wouldn't admit it sober,
but he could even quote a couple of poems by heart. He had
some kind of degree in it. American literature, I think.

Now Lansing looked up. She nodded. She smiled.

"Don't look at me like that, Lansing," I said.

"It's good stuff," she said quietly. Have I mentioned her
eyes? They're blue. And they were sort of wider and softer
just then.

I growled at her: "I'm forty-five. They call me Pops."

"Forget it," said McKay, tossing the paper aside. "Alex
is seventeen. He calls *me* Pops. He saw it in a movie."

I started to put my arms behind my head. The pain in
my shoulder stopped me.

"What is that, anyway?" said Lansing.

"Age," I said.

"Oh, it is not."

"All right. A woman stabbed me with a sharpened stake."

"Oh God. When?"

"I was with the *Gazette* upstate. I was twenty-five. You
were four."

"Why'd she stab you?" said McKay.

"I was trying to keep her from killing her husband."

"What'd she want to do that for?"

"He shot her lover with a bow and arrow."

"Oh."

"Then he began stalking her, hunting her, see, through the woods. But she turned the tables on him. When I showed up, she had him trussed up with a vine at the bottom of a ditch. That's where the sharpened stake came in. Stop looking at me like that, Lansing."

"Shut up, Wells. I'll look how I please."

McKay, who tends to say something stupid when he's embarrassed, said: "They sure don't make them like you anymore, John."

"Yeah," I said, rubbing my shoulder. "That must be why it's so tough to get replacement parts."

That made Lansing and McKay laugh. Cambridge, who had just come in, was reaching for the door to his office when he heard them laugh. He turned. He saw us gathered by my desk across the room. I guess by now I had my feet up on the little filing cabinet at the edge of my cubby. Maybe my jacket was off, too, and my shirt a little rumpled. My tie could possibly have been undone. And I was smoking. Cambridge doesn't like smoking. He's only thinking of me.

So Lansing and McKay laughed, and this caught the attention of Robert Cambridge. He and his snappy brown suit and his tight-lipped smile came wandering up the aisles between the cubbyholes. Their low walls make a mazelike pattern throughout the huge expanse of the city room. They gleam white under the low ceiling of fluorescent lights. At the center of the maze is a long desk where the city editor and the assignment editor sit and chat and laugh. The reporters and the lower rung of editors sit in the cubbyholes under the fluorescent lights and tap at the keyboards of their computer terminals. Except I was sitting in my cubbyhole under the fluorescent lights and I had my feet up. And I don't even have a computer terminal. I have a typewriter. An Olympia Standard. In fact, I was leaning back against my Olympia Standard typewriter when Cambridge reached me. He gave me a good long dose of his tight-lipped smile. He had his leather folder with him too. He caressed it. A bad sign.

And he said: "Hey, guys, how's it goin? What's so all-fired funny around here?" Cambridge is a regular guy. You can tell by the way he talks.

We all murmured: "Bob."

Cambridge waited. "Well?"

"Oh . . ." Lansing smiled. She's good at that. She hoped it would help. "Oh, Wells was just telling one of his stories," she said. "You know."

"Yeah," said Cambridge, with an I-know shake of the head. "Nothing like those great yarns from an old pro, is there." He tapped me on the knee with his folder. Somehow, I was suddenly reminded of the fact that at forty-five I am only a reporter, whereas Cambridge is a managing editor at thirty-two. I don't know what made that pop into my mind.

"Listen, Johnny," said Cambridge. He calls me Johnny because my name is John and he is a regular guy. "You got some free time, right?"

I grinned. I tried to look as if I were eating shit. I don't think it worked.

"Well, I have the Dellacroce trial starting Monday. . . ." I said.

Cambridge wrinkled his finely chiseled nose. He brushed the Dellacroce trial aside with a well-manicured hand.

"Forget it," he said. "Carey can cover that. It's not relatable."

I didn't argue. If it wasn't relatable, it wasn't relatable. Cambridge was hired, after all, to make the *Star* more relatable, which means people will be able to relate to it more. It's a Californian word, I think. They'd brought Cambridge in from a California rag, and it seemed like the word had come with him. In the six months since he'd been here, I'd heard him use it maybe four hundred times. Maybe five. "Johnny," he said to me once on a pretty typical day, "let's concentrate a little less on this mob stuff, this corruption stuff. It's not relatable. We want something like, well . . . don't the pols in this city use prostitutes, right? We could sneak into some high-class whorehouse, right? Take a hidden camera in. Click. I love it. That's relatable."

"Nah," I told him. "I'd be recognized. Anyway, I'm no good at that stuff. I cover courts. Cops. Politics when it's dirty."

8

"Oh, Johnny, Johnny." And he actually wagged his finger at me. "That's not relatable."

So that was three times in one day. For six months. And he was beginning to feel I was not being totally cooperative with him. Perelman used to feel pretty much the same way when he was Cambridge. He was hired to give the *Star* zing. He accused me of deliberately not being zingy. Before that was Davis. He was hired to give the *Star* pizzazz. I can't remember the name of the guy who was Cambridge before that. But now, Cambridge was Cambridge. And Cambridge, I think, had this funny notion that one of us—him or me— was going to have to crack on the issue of relatability. It had become a personal thing with him. So I didn't argue.

"Okay," I said. "What's relatable?"

He glanced at Lansing and McKay with the appeal-to-heaven grin of one really regular guy. "It's sort of like what we discuss in staff meetings once a week," he said. "Look . . . are you familiar at all with what's going on in Grant County?"

I had been smirking. I stopped. "No," I lied.

He snorted, shook his head. "I mean, that's a story, Johnny. That's what we mean when we say a relatable story."

"What's happening in Grant County?" Lansing asked.

Cambridge tapped his folder with his hand. "Teen suicides!"

Lansing audibly drew in her breath. McKay turned away and looked at the floor. They knew about me. Both of them knew. And Cambridge. This is the business of unearthing secrets. Its gossips are pros. No one can hide much for long.

Cambridge went on eagerly. "It started farther north, in Edmond. Ten teenagers up there killed themselves in the last eight months. But now it's hit Grant: In the past six weeks, three students at Grant Valley High School have killed themselves. In the past six weeks. Great story."

I sat and stared at Cambridge. He stared back. I took a long drag on my cigarette and let the smoke out at him in a steady stream.

"I think this is worth a series, maybe even a week with a Sunday finish. I mean real hard-hitting stuff. You-and-me stuff. With all the big questions. Is it a national trend? Is it due to the lack of morality in our society? Is it drugs? Is it sex? The whole thing. How does it affect you-and-me? Just keep saying that to yourself, Johnny. How does it affect you-and-me?"

How does it affect you-and-me? I said to myself.

"Hey," said Lansing aloud. Her eyes glistened—a hard, metallic glisten. "Hey, that sounds just like my kind of assignment, Bob. How about letting me have that one, and then Wells can cover—"

"I want Johnny on it." Cambridge said it quietly, but Lansing knew when to shut up too. The man's eyes were trained on me. His thin smile was even thinner than before. I can't swear to it, but I think he was breathing rapidly with excitement. This wasn't a sudden whim of his. He'd been waiting to catch me with my jacket off, my feet up.

"Grant County's kind of far away for our readership, isn't it?" said McKay softly. I silently thanked him for that. It was downright gallant of him, considering. McKay had a baby to feed. I'd gone to his apartment a few times to see it. It was small with a scrunched-up face and it cried a lot. But he was sort of attached to it. It also liked to eat. Daddy needed his job.

Cambridge, though, was too intent on me to notice Daddy much. "Well," he said dreamily, "I guess Johnny will just have to learn to use the computer in our White Plains bureau. He can send his stories from there. Then he can finally get rid of that typewriter. . . ."

The Olympia was sort of a sticking point.

When Cambridge walked away, I snuffed my cigarette in my coffee cup. It had burned down to the filter. I'd kept it going as long as I could.

Lansing and McKay watched Cambridge go. They waited until the door to his office closed behind him.

"What a bastard," McKay muttered.

"Forget it, Mac," I said.

Lansing's eyes were sharp and angry. Her cheeks were flaming. But she kept her voice quiet and tight. "Why did you let him do that? Why'd you let him get away with it?"

I shrugged.

"You don't have to take it, Wells."

10

"Maybe."

"You know you don't. You're the best crime man in the city."

"Well." I laughed. "There is that."

"You've kept us ahead on every mob story for months. You've broken your back on the Dellacroce trial. Everyone in the paper knows it. The people upstairs too."

"Maybe."

"It isn't fair."

"Maybe."

"Stop saying that."

"It's just a story, Lancer. I've done a lot of them."

She looked at me for a long time with those blue eyes. She looked at me hard. But when she spoke next, her tone was gentle: "You don't have to do it, Wells."

I smiled at her. "Maybe," I said.

She lowered her gaze.

The two of them stood around a while longer. McKay shuffled his feet. Lansing just studied hers. Both of them cursed at Cambridge some more. Both of them agreed: The assignment stank. Then, after a while, they drifted away. Back to their desks. Back to their work. Which was just as well.

I lit another cigarette. I stuck it between my lips. I leaned back with my head against my laced hands.

I thought about Cambridge. I thought about Grant County. I thought about the trapdoor.

2

It had been a while since I'd thought about that: about the trapdoor. But now I couldn't get it out of my mind. I thought about it dropping open with a sudden thud. I could see the blur of the body falling through it. I could see her dangling there.

It was the same that Monday when I drove to Grant County. It kept playing itself out in my mind again and again as I tooled my ancient red Dart—the Artful Dodge—up Interstate 84. It was a bright morning, early in November. The hills of trees had become hills of color. Overlapping swells of red and yellow and light green rose away into the haze of the horizon outside the car windows. The highway was clear. The air was fresh and bracing. The city was over fifty miles behind me.

And I kept thinking about a trapdoor.

At first I'd see her at the bottom of the stairs, her face uplifted to the scaffold. Her expression seemed calm to me, but somehow empty, as if she were under some irresistible spell. She was wearing a robe the color of port wine. Her hair was as I remembered it, thick and golden. I'd see her gray eyes sparkle a little as she reached the platform, as if she were about to awaken and run. But she didn't run. The noose was lowered over her head, tightened around her neck.

My heart raced as I drove through the lovely countryside. I turned the radio on, loud, to drown it out. I tried to shake myself out of it. Nothing worked. In another minute I'd hear the trapdoor snap open. I'd see her fall through. My hands would tighten on the steering wheel. I'd see her dangling in the air before me.

It hadn't been this bad in over a year. I hadn't thought

it would ever be this bad again. The assignment stank, that was the long and the short of it. It stank, and it was supposed to stink. That was Cambridge's idea.

Lansing was right, probably. I could have turned it down. Like she says, I have the leverage these days, and the Dellacroce trial was mine. Maybe it was pride that made me keep my mouth shut, maybe I just didn't want Cambridge to see me quail. Or maybe it was just that Cambridge is the boss and you don't show the boss up over a few personal demons. I'm not sure. Whatever the reason, I'd taken the story. And with the story came the trapdoor. The trapdoor and the port-red robe and the dazed gray eyes and the shadow of the scaffold. The noose. The drop. The dangling girl. Again and again, it played itself over as I drove to Grant County.

Which was kind of strange in a way, really. I mean, my daughter hanged herself, all right. Five years ago. But it wasn't like that at all.

3

My hotel was called the Mountain Inn. It was a rustic lodge set high in the autumn hills. My room was enormous and paneled with pine. It had a double bed, a dresser, an easy chair, and a writing desk with a mirror on it. It also had a large picture window that looked out on the vast forests to the west. Quite a view. A thin layer of mist made the sky smoky and aqua. Beneath it layer after layer of pastel leaves sloped away into the valleys. I could see a lake on the farthest hill. It gleamed silver in the morning sun. I could also see a housing development over there. It gleamed too: Its windows caught the light. The only thing that marred the vista was the scar of an office park that was going up in the woods near the foot of the hill. It was a great brown gash where the trees had been torn away but not replanted, and the ground had been broken but not resown.

As it turned out, a lot of that kind of thing was happening in Grant County just now. For a long time it had been an exurban area, too far for the commute into New York. It had managed to hover on the edge of the urban sprawl. The ravenous developers eyed it and drooled, but for the most part they were kept at bay. About a year ago, though, the railroad had begun to transform the steamline up here to electricity. It was going to take a while for them to lay the lines this far, but when they did, it would cut as much as a half hour off the ride to the city. The suburbanites were already on their way. Just the pioneers now, but the rest were coming. The businesses and the business parks—they were coming too. Land values were soaring. The developers were moving in.

I could see it as I drove the Artful Dodge down from the hotel. At the bottom of the hotel's mountain, just beneath the office park I'd noticed under construction—Capstandard, it was called—there was a low-lying swampland. The sound of peepers, bullfrogs, and crickets grew loud for a few moments as my car wheeled by. A sign told me the area was protected by the county. I glanced through my window at the scar of the Capstandard office park above. The county's protection wouldn't mean much once the sewage from the park started running downhill.

I wound my way around the mountain's base. On the other side, opposite the park, was an old graveyard: a collection of monuments rolling back up the slope. Old slabs leaning this way and that, washed clean of their inscriptions by time. I was fairly certain the bodies beneath them had been buried sometime in the seventeenth century. And across the street, on the slope of the opposing hill, was a collection of imitation Tudor houses in a development called King Henry's Court. I was passing through a county at odds with itself.

I cruised slowly toward the center of the town of Grant Valley, the county seat. I drove on winding roads. Thin roads already rutted with the early rains. Forests crowded the edge of the pavement on every side. If you didn't look carefully, you'd have thought you were in the middle of nowhere. But behind the trees, in every forest along the way, bulldozers squatted like dinosaurs. You could see them now that the leaves were falling. You could see the brown gashes they'd ripped in the earth, and the heartless faces of new houses poured straight from the package. Where the woods were still intact, you could see For Sale signs growing up on the forest edges like the little sprigs that bloom under giant pines.

I drove on. The forests receded. Pleasant houses sat among the trees: old, sturdy clapboards, most of them with porches and porch swings. Basketball hoop up on the garage. Mama's old car parked under it. Papa's newer car away at the office. A rake leaning on a wall.

Sometimes you saw a woman hanging up laundry on a backyard line. Sometimes you saw a woman hauling groceries from the car's rear trunk to the house's front door. Sometimes you saw a golden retriever or an Irish setter or a collie snoozing on the lawn. Almost always you saw a bike or a tricycle lying on its side somewhere.

I'd come about five miles from the hotel now. The woods were gone altogether, or wrestled back, anyway, into the hills that rose all around. The houses were larger here but closer to one another. Instead of woods, they were surrounded by trim little lawns. The cars in the garages were bigger than those I'd seen before. There were still bicycles and basketball hoops, but swing sets, too, and sandboxes, and even a jungle gym here and there.

I came to a traffic light—the first I had seen. It was at an intersection where the winding road ended and a wider, straighter street crossed its path. The light changed and I turned right. I had arrived in the center of town.

Main Street. Offices, groceries, gas stations, and convenience stores. A fire house and a medical building. A two-story brick town hall, and a four-story concrete county hall. There were sidewalks now. Parking meters, parking spaces. Cars—at intervals—passing back and forth. Around the next corner was a tiny mall, and next to that a community center. There was a liquor store, a radio store, a toy store, an Army recruitment office. The whole thing took up only a few blocks. The hills hung above them everywhere.

The high school sat at the very top of the road, on the left side of an intersection. There was a parking lot beside it. I pulled in.

I got out and looked up at the place. It was your standard federal schoolhouse: the one in the textbooks, the one on TV. Two stories of brick, then the wooden white dome on top. The clock under the dome and the dome capped by the wind cock.

There were no kids to be seen. None on the front steps. None on the track and athletics yard around the other side. The cars on the road behind me whispered as they rolled past. There were two maple trees on the school's front yard, and their dying leaves whispered too. Aside from those whispers, the place was awfully quiet. The windows were dark, and the whole soul of the place seemed hunkered in on itself. It seemed a somber place amid the autumn brightness.

I glanced up at the clock under the dome. It was nearly eleven. I was right on time. The memorial service for the children was about to begin.

4

The principal's name was David Brandt. He was a tall man, trim but broad-shouldered. He had red hair and blue eyes in a pale, handsome face. He was forty, maybe, but a young forty. The vigorous type. He came out of his office to meet me. I was standing in front of the glass panel before the receptionist. Brandt pushed out through the door beside the panel, and a golden retriever trotted out with him. The retriever sniffed my leg and panted. I patted the retriever's head.

"This is Sosh," said Brandt. His handshake winded me. It was one of those firm, sincere, take-charge handshakes. He looked me dead in the eye when he shook my hand. He had a firm, deep, take-charge voice too. "Sort of the campus dog. Wandered into a Social Studies class a few years ago and has stayed ever since." He dropped my hand and strode to the door. "She guards the place at night, and roams free during the day. Sort of our mascot."

And with a gesture, he was gone—out into the hall. The dog followed him. I followed the dog.

We walked between rows of metal lockers separated by wooden classroom doors.

"I'm glad you could be here for the service. I think it's important for you to get a sense of how the school is dealing with this. I'm going to make a few remarks—sort of personal reminiscences about those we've lost. Then Reverend Jacobsen will be speaking, and Dr. Carter. She's a psychologist we've taken on staff." I could hear the dog's toenails clicking on the floor tiles. Brandt set a rapid pace. "The idea of the memorial itself . . . well, after the first tragedy—Nancy's— we simply found it necessary to give the kids . . . something.

Let them know we cared and we were all in this together. Give them a chance to share their grief. Of course, we didn't know there'd be so much grief to share."

We came around a corner. A narrowing corridor lay before me. Gun-metal lockers. Wooden doors with narrow glass windows on them. The pink water fountains too low to the ground. The green tiles of the floor. The pink tiles of the wall. Every high school in America must look the same.

Brandt kept talking. He spoke forcefully. He gestured with his hand as he walked. His voice sounded sincere. The look in his eyes was solemn but hopeful. He told me about his programs. He told me about grief. He told me about the death of children.

I walked along beside him, my hands in my pants pocket, my eyes on my shoes. I remembered sitting on the porch with my father. He was leaning back in his chair with his feet up on the rail. So was I. He was smoking a Winston. So was I. I was seventeen. Tall and broad and ugly as he was.

"Hey, Pop," I said. "Let me ask you something."

"Shoot."

"Does life ever get any better than high school?"

He laughed. "Hell, yes. Hell, yes. Hell of a lot worse too."

Brandt came to a stop. He stood before the double doors of the auditorium. He smoothed down the front of his jacket with one hand and reached for the knob with the other.

"Did you know any of them?" I said.

He glanced at me quickly. "What's that?"

"Did you know any of them personally?"

He reared back a little. "I know all my students personally."

He glanced away from me. Still, I had seen it. It had risen in his blue, take-charge eyes like a body from the bottom of a lake. He wrestled with it, forced it under again. But by then I'd had a good, clear view.

The man was in a state of panic. He was terrified. I wasn't sure why. I guess it was because his kids were dying, and he was establishing programs, and holding services, and hiring shrinks, and he couldn't do a damn thing to make the dying stop. What I saw in his eyes at that moment was a kind of plea. He was begging me: say I'm all right. Write it in your newspaper. Write in your newspaper that I'm a young, vigorous, take-charge kind of guy. Write about our programs and our psychologist. Write that we're handling it. That it's under control. Maybe if it's in the paper, people will believe it. Maybe if people believe it, it will be true.

I guess he was terrified I'd expose him—or maybe expose him to himself. I should have put his mind at rest. If I wanted to write the truth, I'd get out of the newspaper business.

He took a deep breath. I heard the hitch in it. He pulled open the auditorium door. He went in. The dog went in. I went in.

The place was a theater. About six hundred seats fanned out from a low stage. There was a podium on the stage with three wooden chairs behind it. The preacher and the doctor were sitting on two of the chairs. The audience was made up mostly of students, with one or two teachers here and there. A little chaos of young voices died as Brandt came down the center aisle.

It was a grand entrance. He could have just used the stage door. But he was like that: flamboyant, as small-town high school principals go. Popular too. I could tell. The kids' faces turned toward him when he entered. Their eyes fixed on him and held him and wouldn't let him go. He had good reason to panic. They expected a lot of him. He smiled and nodded to them all.

I stayed at the back of the auditorium as he continued down toward the stage. I watched him pause to speak with a student here and there. He would lean toward one of them, lay a hand on a shoulder. Speak in a confidential murmur, pass on.

I watched his progress. And I watched the kids. They looked very young. Many of the girls seemed pale. Some seemed to have been crying. One or two were sobbing outright, their faces in their hands, their shoulders heaving. The boys, also, some of them, looked wan and grim.

I found myself thinking about the letters. The letters my wife got when Olivia died. The ones from the kids she'd known. "Dear Mrs. Wells, I wanted to tell you how sorry . . ." they all began. I read every one of them. Then I read them again. Some of them seemed to me full of spontaneous grief. Some of them were the hysterics of kids who just wanted to be in on the drama. I didn't care. I read them all. In all of them there was something. Grief, or guilt at the absence of grief, or confusion at the absence of guilt, or terror at the absence of confusion. Something in the souls of every one of them to mark the place where my daughter had been.

So then, standing in the auditorium, looking at the kids' faces, thinking about those letters—just then was the first time I gave a damn about the suicides of Grant County. I felt the old juices flow: one part curiosity, two parts habit, three parts the tricks of the trade. I forgot the trapdoor. I pushed it aside. I stood there looking at the mourning faces, and began to consider how to get the story. Nothing else: just how to get the story.

I figured I'd begin with the parents. That would be a good start. I would sit there wearing my serious, sensitive face and ask questions in my quiet, concerned voice. They'd look at me and see a friend, and they'd tell me everything. They'd talk about how bright their kid had been. How sweet and how outgoing. They'd tell me how baffled they were that he or she had decided to put an end to so promising an existence. There was no sign, they'd say. We didn't know, they'd say. We didn't do anything wrong, they'd say. Then they'd probably cry and I'd pat their hands. It makes good copy. It's part of the story.

Next, I figured I'd go to the friends. These kids who were sitting in the theater before me now. Not all of them. Just the ones who were closest to the dead. Just the ones who hurt the most, who'd give the reader the most pain and bewilderment for his thirty-five cents. I'd drop the solemn business then, and come on as the tough guy who's seen it all. Kids usually go for that. They'll spot you if you try to pretend you're one of them. But they usually talk for the tough-guy routine.

I'd finish off with the experts. You've got to have experts or the reader feels he's being conned. Psychologists and Ph.D.s, authors and the like. You can always find someone. For a little ink they come pouring out of the woodwork like beetles. Then all I have to do is get them to say something that makes sense.

Anyway, it figured to be a good little series if the editors kept their hands off it. Lots of anguish, lots of tragedy. Human interest, as it's called. The assignment stank, there was no question about it. But I'd been on worse. I'd seen the bodies of hundreds scattered on a field where a plane went down.

I'd seen three-year-olds scarred with cigarette burns because their mommies got mad. I've watched guys with the IQs of children walk into the gas chamber to gag and die for a crime they couldn't remember. I once interviewed a gentleman who'd tortured fifteen women to death, and when the interview was over, he shook my hand and clapped me on the shoulder. I stayed drunk for a month after that one.

The trick to it is: you think about the story. No trapdoors. No psychology. Just the story. Just get the story. There was no one waiting for me at home, anyway. No one who wanted to. I was too ugly for the love of women, and too mean for the company of friends. My wife had left me, my kid was dead. I was forty-five, and a newspaperman, and that's all I was ever likely to be. I'd get the story, basically, because I had nothing better to do. And I would not think about the trapdoor. I was determined not to think about the trapdoor.

David Brandt mounted the steps of the stage. Sosh, the retriever, went up behind him, her tail wagging. The dog lay down up there, her muzzle on her folded paws. She looked out dully over the edge of the stage for a moment, then closed her eyes and slept.

Brandt took his place behind the podium. Every trace of panic was gone. He was all vigor and sincerity. He spoke briefly about the sad occasion that had brought them together once again, and about how difficult it was to understand. He said they would all stick it out, anyway, and do their best. The kids nodded, and kept their eyes on him. Then Brandt introduced the doctor and the preacher who were sitting behind him. He gestured down the aisle at me.

"The gentleman standing at the back," he said, "is John Wells, a reporter for the New York City *Star*. Mr. Wells is here to do a series of stories on the tragedies that have come to us. Whether or not you cooperate with him is, of course, up to each of you. For myself, I think the more the public learns about this terrible problem, the better."

The students turned in their seats and looked at me. They studied me for several moments. They didn't look particularly happy I was there.

All in all, I couldn't blame them.

5

I was looking at the snapshot of a girl. She was fifteen, small and slender. She had dark skin. Big, serious brown eyes. A pleasant face, but not all that pretty. She had straight hair, dark brown. The kind of hair teenaged girls always wish was fluffy and blond. It hung down long in back.

"She used to chew on it when she was thinking," her mother said.

Her mother's hair had been dark brown, too, but there was a lot of gray in it now. She was a trim, elegant woman. She was wearing a one-piece navy-blue dress, and a single strand of pearls. She held the strand in the fingers of one hand, and with the other reached out to take the snapshot back from me.

Her name was Carla Scofield. The girl in the photograph was her daughter, Nancy. Nancy was dead.

We were sitting in the screened-in porch of the Scofield's colonial home, about a mile from the center of town. The house was at the top of an incline, with the porch overlooking the driveway below. Mrs. Scofield sat on the sofa with the snapshots and mementos fanned out before her on the coffee table. She searched among them with one hand. With the other she fingered the pearls.

She handed me another photo. Nancy playing the clarinet.

"She played in the school band when she was younger. You know, not that badly. Not that well. She practiced, though. I never had to remind her."

She did look very serious about it in the picture. Her

lips frowning over the reed, her brow wrinkled in concentration. Her fingers seemed heavy and deliberate on the stops.

Mrs. Scofield smiled. She smiled a lot. The skin of her high cheekbones pulled taut on her face when she smiled. Her eyes glistened. I looked in her eyes. Then I stopped looking.

Her husband Larry sat beside her on the arm of the sofa. Like her, he was in his early forties. A thin man of medium size with a round, friendly face like his daughter's, topped with a thin halo of reddish hair. He'd taken a half day off from work to talk to me. He worked as a sales executive at IBM. Mrs. Scofield was a full-time mother. She had a ten-year-old boy and a five-year-old girl to care for.

"Was it six weeks ago already?" Mrs. Scofield said. She looked up at her husband. Her bright smile flashed. He nodded. He couldn't look in her eyes either. "It doesn't seem that way. It doesn't seem that way at all. Maybe I'm just not . . . used to the idea."

"Of course you're not," said Mr. Scofield. He patted her shoulder. She showed him part of her smile. "We've joined a group," he told me. "Down in White Plains. A group of parents who've . . . lost children this way. It's very . . . helpful to talk to other people who've been through the same thing."

I nodded. His expression cried out to me: *It's not. It's not helpful at all. Nothing helps. Ever.*

"You have to understand," said Mrs. Scofield, and now there was a tone of urgency in her voice. "It happened on an ordinary day. It seems like . . . if you could just erase that one hour from that one day, then everything would be . . . back to normal again."

"It was the last week of September?" I said.

"Yes. That's right. A Wednesday. Just a week after school began. It was about five-thirty when I came home from the supermarket with Betsy. Brad was in the basement, playing with his trains. Nancy was upstairs. She was . . ." And for the first time, her smile faltered. There was a hitch in her voice. Her husband leaned toward her as if to catch her. But she went on: "She was still alive then."

"She couldn't have known," he explained to me.

"Well, you see, she'd been happier. All summer. Nancy was always a quiet, an introspective girl. She didn't have very many friends. She wasn't dating yet. She always worried about that. She thought she was ugly. She always said her hair . . ." As she spoke, she reached out and touched one of the photos of her daughter on the table. She touched her daughter's hair, as if to set it right. "I told her and told her: her hair was just fine." She glanced up quickly. "But she'd been quite happy all summer. She'd had a job . . . at McDonald's. She'd been . . . looking better. Taking better care of the way she dressed and made up and all. I really couldn't have known . . . I really didn't. . . ."

"Of course you couldn't," said her husband.

Her hand fluttered up in the air like a bird flushed from a hedge. She had meant a quieter gesture, but it got away from her.

"I was down there in the kitchen making dinner all that time. All that time . . . when she was dying," she said. "Even when it was dinnertime, I called to her. She said . . . she said, 'I'm writing something, Mother.' She said, 'I'll eat later.' She called it out from behind the door. I thought it was a school assignment. I didn't want to disturb her."

"Sure," I said.

"You know, my husband and I, we didn't even know she wrote . . . poetry and short stories. We didn't even know until we found them all."

"I'd like to see some of them," I said.

Mrs. Scofield, fingering her pearls, reached into the papers and snapshots spread out before her. She found a piece of looseleaf notepaper and lifted it out from the rest.

"This was what she was writing," she said softly. "When I called in to her. This is what we found when we finally broke down the door. It wasn't until much later that we did it. Bedtime almost. We were all . . . busy. Busy, I . . . I don't know."

"I was watching TV," said Mr. Scofield, as if he were amazed by it. "I was watching an old western on TV. Richard Widmark was in it."

"And I was washing up, and getting the kids ready for bed and . . . It was an ordinary day. Can you understand that? It was an ordinary day." The skin over her cheeks stretched tight with her brittle smile. I told her I could understand. "Even when we finally went up there . . . even when we started knocking, we thought she was asleep. You see? We knocked for ten minutes before we did it, before we finally broke down the door. This is what we found when we went in. She was lying on the bed with her hands folded on her chest. This was in her hands."

I took the paper. The writing on it had been done with a ballpoint pen. It was precise and girlish-clean, with carefully sculpted letters, small and round. It was a poem.

It would make a good ending for the first article in the series:

A VALENTINE
by
Nancy Scofield

Do you consider that I have not seen,
day after day, your moving away from me?
Woven, intrinsic, in the things we've been—
loving and loved—the good-bye must also be.
Life doesn't have a life apart from dying.
No day begins that does not see its night.
No lover knows a love apart from crying.
My tears are darkness. Our love was the light.

And now sunset's coming. And now, the sun's set.
My love has died with it, but not my regret.
Life, too, must be over, before I forget.

I glanced up, about to speak. I didn't speak. Mrs. Scofield spoke first.

"You see," she said, smiling brightly, brightly. "She'd already taken the pills when I first called her. So many pills." She shook her head, smiling. "So many, many pills."

6

So for Nancy Scofield, anyway, life never got any better than high school. But then, I guess it never got any worse either.

For her it had been a life lived in the shadow of a hallway wall. She clung to that shadow as she passed from class to class. She held close to the lines of locker doors as if they rimmed a zone of invisibility through which she could walk unnoticed. Her eyes studied the floor. Her voice, when she was forced into a greeting, was a whisper. In the high school world of cliques and stations, hers was the station of the painfully shy, the clique of the obscure. Like the song says, nobody knew she was there.

And then, one day, she wasn't. *Life doesn't have a life apart from dying.* That's the way she wrote it. A queer little poem. I'd have to show it to McKay when I got back to the city. He'd told me once—when we'd had a couple in Flanagan's place—something Nathaniel Hawthorne said. Something like: You can spend your whole life trying to understand the things you write when you're young. Nancy's poem reminded me of that. It was written by a girl who had thought dark thoughts—and then stepped off the edge of things before she'd had time to come to grips with the darkness.

Lonely as she was, she did have two close friends. Her clique of three. The ones she talked to about guys and life and, as it turned out, death too. Joanne was a fat, unattractive girl. Fifteen. She had pimples on her plump cheeks. She had short mousy hair that dangled limply. Mindy, on the other hand, was small and pert-looking. She'd already developed a good figure. She wore her jeans tight in back and her sweater tight in front to show it off. She had a round face which was not beautiful. But she had nice, big eyes—pale brown—and her slightly buck teeth gave her a cute, squirrelly look.

I met them in back of the school as the day ended. In front the kids were filing to their yellow buses, or drifting in groups down the tree-lined sidewalks. To the side of the red-brick building the teams were pouring out onto the track. Boys in shorts and sweatshirts. Girls in sweatshirts and culottes. The kids bent and stretched on the lawn surrounding the asphalt track. The voices of coaches drifted to us where we stood.

It had gotten colder. I was cold, anyway, even though I wore my heavy overcoat and kept my hands shoved in the pockets. I had a cigarette clenched between my teeth. Smoke and vapor came out on my breath together. I walked between Mindy and Joanne into the schoolyard.

Mostly, it was a broad square of grass, bordered by low slopes and fences. There were little elm and oak trees planted here and there. Only the far end was wide open for use as a playing field. There were soccer nets set up there.

But there was one corner of the place that was not grass, that had been paved over and fenced in. It was a little picnic area. Two maple trees overhung the tables and benches. The open asphalt had a dodgeball court painted on it. There was a tetherball pole to one side. The little area was empty now. The yellow leaves of the maples were falling into it. They blew across the pavement in the chill wind.

We stood in a row of three, looking through the fence.

"She used to always be out here," Mindy told me. It was clear she had been the leader of the group. "She used to always be out here reading." Her voice was hard. She was chewing gum. Her big brown eyes stared impassively.

Joanne nodded. "Yeah," she said. She was chewing gum as well.

"She used to read all this morbid stuff," Joanne continued. "Poetry. You know what I mean? Like, always about death."

"Was it?"

"Yeah, yeah. Go ahead. You can write that down." I kept standing there with my hands in my pockets. "No, really, it was. Ask Joanne," Mindy said.

"It was," said Joanne.

"You know, like Edgar Allen Poe, or Emily Dickinson or somebody. Then she'd write these stories and show them to you." Mindy shivered. She was wearing a scarf, but she kept her shocking pink flight jacket open to show off the front of her sweater. "Jesus. They were always about some person, you know, breaking up with someone or something, and it always ended . . . they either took pills or put their heads in the oven or blew their brains out or something." She glanced at me, a little pleadingly behind all that grit, I thought. "We always thought they were kind of funny," she said.

I nodded, bit down on my cigarette. The cigarette smoked and burned in the cold, clear air. I pictured Nancy out there for a second. At the picnic table. Her arms folded over the top of a book, her head bent down over it. Long hair dangling. Maybe a strand of it in her mouth.

"Any of it true?" I asked.

"Like what?" said Mindy.

"Yeah, like what?" said Joanne.

"Did she have a boyfriend or anything? Someone she broke up with."

"Nancy?" Mindy shook her head wisely. "You gotta be joking. Only in her dreams. I mean all she could ever talk about was, 'I'm too flat-chested, my hair's too limp, I'm ugly, I'm stupid,' I'm this and that."

"She used to get angry at me when I told her it didn't matter," said Joanne, almost to herself.

"Yeah," said Mindy, "she was always saying, like, 'I might as well be dead.' I used to try to tease her out of it, you know. I mean, jokingly . . . You know what I mean? Not seriously. Just as a joke. I think she used to like it. Really," she said.

I finally said, "Sure. I understand."

"Yeah," said Mindy, relieved. "Yeah." Then she bit her lip and looked down at the ground.

"But her mother told me she was a little more cheerful this summer."

"Yeah," said Mindy. "Yeah. She was."

"So I thought, maybe, you know, she'd met a guy."

Mindy considered it. Glanced at me, shook her head.

"Nah. We'd have known. We would've. I mean, if you read her stories and stuff, you'd think she never did anything but have lovers and kill herself. . . ." Her voice trailed away. She looked down at the ground again.

"So what was it, you think," I asked quietly. "What made her happier, before the end?"

"I . . . I don't know, what was I, her shrink or something?" She raised her eyes defiantly for a moment. But only for a moment. "I mean, it was summer," she said then. "I guess. I guess that was it. I mean, she was out of here, out of this lousy place. Jesus, that would cheer anyone up."

I nodded. "Okay. Then what? What turned the screw?"

Mindy kept looking down, kept shaking her head. "Life," she said. "That's all. Just life. It sucks."

"Yeah," said Joanne. "It really does."

I plucked the cigarette from my mouth, darted it into the grass at my feet. "Yeah, well, I guess that would do it," I said.

The irony was faint, but Mindy heard it. "Well, maybe it was different back when you were a kid," she said. Her voice was soft now. The corner of her lips were pulled down in a frown. "But for us, okay, it stinks. I mean, everybody says, oh, you know, 'Why do kids take drugs, why are they so fucked up, why do they get pregnant, why do they kill themselves?' And the television and everybody interviews the parents and the teachers and the experts and maybe the kids who tow the company line, the good little boys and girls, you know. But lookit: on the one side, we've got a bunch of idiot teachers who can't do anything else and are probably afraid to do anything else or whatever, and their biggest thrill, you know, is telling us what to do, when, if you ask me, any girl who can have a goddamned baby ought to be able to decide when to chew gum or not. And on the other hand, you got a bunch of kids, they care about looking cool and getting laid and getting into college and being on the football team and making money, you know. And I'll go out with you but not with you, and you can come to my party and you can't, and you're not one of us, you know. And then, I mean, the worst thing is, the fucking worst thing of all is: it stays this way. I mean, doesn't it? Basically, I mean, that's what life is like.

It's idiots telling you what to do on one side, and everyone fighting to be, like, more popular or rich or something on the other. So why don't you write that in your story: 'Nancy Scofield killed herself because we run a fucked-up world and high school is where we teach kids to live in it'?"

She shook her head violently. Her chestnut hair tossed back and forth. She snapped her gum.

"I used to tell Nancy," she went on fiercely, "I used to tell her: what do you want to be like those girls for, turning their noses up at everybody? I mean, they go out with those idiot guys, all they can talk about is 'Oh, yeah, man, I'm a jock, aren't I cool,' or what record they bought. I mean, that's what she wanted to be like. I told her—" said Mindy. Then she burst into tears.

She turned her face away from me. Inside her shocking pink flight jacket her shoulders shook. I could hear the sobs rack her.

"You fuck," she managed to say at last. "All of you. All of you fucking people." She cried and cried, moaning. "Why didn't somebody help her? That's what I want to know, all right? All right? I mean, if all you fucking old people are so smart, all right? Why didn't one of you help her?"

7

It was Tuesday night. I was in my hotel room on the mountaintop. I was at the writing desk with the mirror on it. My portable electric typewriter was set up in front of me. There was a glassful of scotch to the left of it. There was an ashtray full of smoldering butts to the right.

I pounded at the keys. The Scofield story was nearly done. Cambridge wasn't planning to run the first piece in the series until Sunday. Then he'd follow-up Monday, Wednesday, and Friday, and wrap the thing with a big piece the Sunday following. I could get the piece finished tonight, express it down to the paper tomorrow morning, and never go near the computer terminal in White Plains.

The sound of the clacking keys was comforting in the lonely room. The scotch made my belly warm. The smoke from my latest cigarette curled and twisted up around my nose. It smelled good. The page rolled up before me. Another 'graph, maybe two, it would be finished.

The picture window was to my right, the bathroom to my left. The bathroom door was closed now. Someone was in there. I could hear her, even as I typed. She was getting ready. I could hear the legs of the chair scraping against the tiled floor as she dragged it over. But I kept typing.

Outside, there was lightning. No thunder, just jagged daggers of white light above the trees. I glanced at the window when I saw a flash. For an instant I could make out the slope of grass leading away from the room to the edge of the forest below. The grass and the forest leaves, and the tree branches: all of them shone silver before the night closed on them again.

I kept typing. The page rolled upward. I could hear wood scraping in the bathroom. She was nearly done. But before she finished, there came a tapping at the window. A light tapping, as of someone hitting his fingernail against the glass.

Startled, I turned toward the window. The lightning forked through the sky again. For the briefest second the slope went silver with light. And in that second I saw—or thought I saw—a figure standing just beyond the edge of the woods. It seemed to me to be a woman, cowled in black. But the lightning was gone so fast, I could only believe I had imagined her, created her from a shadow thrown by the trees.

I went on typing. I had to hurry. I wanted to be finished before she was done in the bathroom. It was quiet in there. I knew I didn't have much time.

The tapping came at the window again.

I turned. The lightning flashed. The cowled woman now stood nearer, halfway between the woods and the window. For a single instant I had a glimpse of her. Of her pale face.

The dark returned, and she was gone. I cursed and got out of my chair. I went to the window. I was confused, and a little afraid. She couldn't have come that far up from the woods in the time between the flashes. It seemed impossible. There was one loud scrape of wood in the bathroom. I ignored it and went to the window.

I pressed my nose to the pane. I could see the vague outline of the grass, the vague shadows of the trees. I could not find her figure among them.

The lightning flashed and she was standing directly before me, her pale face pressed to the opposite side of the glass, her dead eyes staring into mine, her sad smile almost kissing me.

I cried out, and fell back from her. It was my daughter. It was Olivia. Slowly, she raised her hand to me. She pointed to the bathroom door.

I turned. I rushed to the door. It was too late. I had known all along it would be too late. I grabbed the knob and pulled it. It wouldn't budge. I pounded on the door. I screamed: "Olivia!"

She laughed. I could hear her, in the bathroom, giggling brightly. I could hear her footsteps. She was climbing up the scaffold. She was up on it, fitting the rope around her neck. Tightening it. Placing herself within the lines of the trapdoor.

I shrieked her name again. And I sat up on the bed, shrieking it. I woke up, panting. My face ran with sweat.

I sat on the edge of the bed. I bowed my head into my hands and moaned softly. I waited while my heartbeat eased.

For a few moments the broken strands of the dream hung in my mind like cobwebs. I remembered I'd lay down to rest for a while. But I was not sure when reality had eased into nightmare, or when nightmare had become all there was.

I stood up, rubbing my eyes. I was still dressed. My clothes felt rank. I glanced at my watch. It was half past midnight. I looked around me.

The typewriter was on the desk before the mirror. The scotch glass, the ice all melted into the pale amber, stood to its left. The ashtray to its right was filled with dead butts. The room stank of stale smoke.

The Scofield piece sat neatly on top of the typewriter. It was done. I began to move toward it. But I paused on the way, stood in the center of the room transfixed and glanced toward the picture window.

There was no lightning. Only mist. I'd been told there was always mist around here at night. Something to do with the large number of lakes. Tonight there was a gibbous moon, and it made the mist electric, filled it with light. I could see it snaking around the trunks of the trees at the edge of the forest. I could see it breathing—rising and falling slowly—where it lay on the slope.

I turned away and went to the typewriter. I stood and reread my lead. It looked okay. I raised my eyes and saw myself in the mirror. I didn't look so good.

I'd slept in my best white shirt. It was a sorry sight. It was soaked with sweat at the chest, the armpits, and the collar. Sweat was still finding trails down the furrows of my face. It beaded on my forehead below the high hairline and in the dark circles beneath my eyes. My eyes looked very weary. And afraid.

When I couldn't look anymore, I went into the bathroom. I flicked on the light and went to the sink. I ran the water until it got cold. I bent to it. I caught it in my cupped hands. I splashed it over my face.

It felt good. I stood there a moment, enjoying the cold. I took a towel from the rack and dried myself. Then I stopped and stood still. I closed my eyes tight. My heart beat fast again.

Someone was tapping at the window.

8

I stood there another moment. The tapping contin-ued. I stood there, as if I were waiting to wake up again. It did no good. Softly but steadily the sound kept on. A harsh, staccato rhythm: tap-tap-tap, tap-tap, tap-tap-tap. I just stood there, the towel in my hand. I told myself that it was not my daughter, tapping like that. Hovering in the cold, at the window. Asking me to let her in. I was not asleep anymore. My daughter was dead. And they don't come back, the dead. No matter what old score needs to be settled.

But the tapping went on. I drew a breath. I tossed the towel over the edge of the sink. I came out of the bathroom.

As I crossed the threshold, the tapping ceased. It ceased abruptly. The sudden silence startled me. Slowly, I turned to face the window. The night was out there. The white mist wafted over the surface of the night. Tendrils of the mist reached out to me, caressed the glass. Nothing else. No one.

I went to the desk. My pack of Winstons lay next to the ashtray. I picked it up, jerked a butt into my hand. My hand was shaking. I put the cigarette between my lips and lit a match.

I saw the match flare twice. Once before me as I raised it to the tip of the 'rette, and again—out of the corner of my eye—reflected on the dark pane of the picture window. I waved the match out. Another light flashed in the window. Again I saw it out of the corner of my eye.

I looked up quickly. For a split second the light stayed on. It was a flashlight, I guess. It made a little globe of illumination in the mist, about fifteen yards down the slope. There was a figure floating within that globe.

34

The light was gone. Like the dream lightning, it vanished in an instant. But I'd seen the figure, transparent, shifting, like the mist itself. It had been a person dressed in white— white pants, white shirt. White face. I could not tell whether it was a man or a woman.

As I stared, the light flashed again. The figure was still there, still floating ghostly in the mist. I squinted to get a better view. It was no good. The light went out. The figure was gone.

"All right," I said. My heart was pounding, high up in my throat it seemed. I plucked the cigarette from my mouth, stubbed it out roughly in the ashtray. I went to the front door.

I was on the first floor of the hotel. My room jutted out of the body of the place, forming a little corner of its own. The door opened directly onto the outside, onto a slate path under the balcony of the second story. In one direction the path led to the hotel office. In the other it curled around the corner, past other rooms and along the rim of the slope under my picture window.

I stepped out into a clean chill. The air was damp and thick with the mist, rich with the smell of the dead autumn leaves.

I moved toward the edge of the wooden wall. I kept close to the wall as I went, kept in the shadow of the balcony above me. After I turned the corner, I stood very still. It was quiet. The hotel was dark. The night seemed lifeless and empty. The insect voice of the woods was dim. The mist floated before me, full of shadows. The shadows grew and shrank and shifted on the bed of moonlight.

I heard it then. A footstep on the fallen leaves on the slope below. I heard another and another. They were moving away from me. Down the slope. Toward the woods.

I followed.

I stepped into the open, out of the protection of the balcony. I stepped into the mist and the quiet. I moved gingerly down the slope. It wasn't sharp, but the leaves beneath my feet felt slick and slippery.

I was halfway between the hotel and the woods when I stopped. I couldn't hear the footsteps anymore. I couldn't see the hotel behind me. I couldn't see the forest ahead. There was nothing—nothing but the mist and the low, secret hum of the insects around me.

The light flashed again. The figure was there, standing at the edge of the forest now, just within the first row of trees, just where my daughter had been when I first saw her in the dream. The figure had paused and was gazing back at me. It was a steady gaze. I saw the light reflected in its fathomless black eyes.

I followed. The light went out. Again I heard footsteps, moving away. I quickened my pace. I saw the vapor of my breath spiral out ahead of me, mingling with the mist. I felt my lungs working hard in my chest. I felt the cigarettes. All the cigarettes. I was nearly running.

In another moment I was surrounded by the forest. The trees rushed past me: obscure, half-buried shapes. The angle of the slope seemed to increase under me. The leaves grew slicker. Suddenly my feet skidded. My arms pinwheeled. I reached out, touched nothing. I nearly went down. Finally, my knees bent, I found my footing, regained my balance. I stood still, breathing hard.

And I heard a footstep just beside me.

I swung to face it. There was the figure's silhouette— not ten feet away.

Neither of us moved. "What do you want?" I wondered if I could be heard over the sound of my heart.

A light, high voice answered me. I thought it was a woman's—then a man's—then a boy's.

It said: "I want to show you, Mr. Wells . . . I want to show you that death is in these woods."

And with that the figure faded back into the mist. Just drifted away from me, losing its substance as it went. I rushed after it, reaching for it, but took hold of nothing. The thing was gone.

Now I moved through the darkness slowly, baffled. I'd heard no footsteps, I'd seen no motion but that slight gesture of fading back. I'd been within steps of the creature, and it had slipped away from me. I reached out before me in disbelief. I reached out, moving my hand back and forth in the shifting tendrils.

36

I reached out . . . and my fingers brushed against something. Something that was dead.

I knew it was dead right away. I felt the bloated tautness of it. My hand sprung back. I heard a creaking noise. A twisted, grotesque body swung toward me out of the mist. It was hung from a rope. It was dangling from the branch of a tree. It swung slowly away from me until it vanished in the fog. It twisted on the rope as it swung. It swung back toward me until I could see it again.

It was Sosh. It was the high school dog.

9

Which is how I met Tammany Bird.

He was an impressive figure. Somewhere between sixty and immortal; the size of a building, the shape of an egg. He was chief of the Grant County police department, and he looked like he'd been a cop since the world began. He had a long, sad face with a putty nose and eyes the color of a pane of glass. He was bald but for a fringe of yellowish hair. His hands, his arms, his fingers, his legs: everything about him was oversized; huge. Everything but his voice, which was a soft, easy drawl, nearly a whisper.

Chief Bird arrived about twenty minutes after I called the cops. It was about 1:35 in the morning then. He pulled up in the hotel cul-de-sac in a red-and-white cruiser, its flashers whirling. He unfolded himself from the backseat like a circus trick. He brushed the wrinkles off the front of his dark suit. Two uniformed officers got out of the car's front. They waited for Tammany Bird to lead them. He looked around leisurely once—a long, slow sweep of the eyes that took in everything. Then he led them over the slate walkway, to the corner room, to me.

I was waiting for him in the doorway.

"You John Wells?" he drawled.

"That's me."

"You're the reporter up from the city."

I was surprised he knew me. I tried not to show it. "Yeah," was all I said.

He nodded his big head. He gave me one of his slow studies. I guessed he had about as much use for a reporter up from the city as he did for, say, a poke in the eye with a sharp stick. That was fine with me. I was cold. I was tired.

38

I was shaken. Nothing puts me in a bum mood like being dragged out of my room and into the woods to find a hanging dog. It's just the kind of thing that kills my patience for hick cops.

I took them down into the forest to the victim.

Bird and his men had powerful flashlights. They cut a path for us through the mist. The light etched the dead retriever sharply where it hung from a sturdy oak branch. Bird took a look at it. He sucked his lips once against his teeth. Then he drawled softly, "Okay. Cut the poor bitch down."

The officers glanced at each other. One was a thin blond fellow in his early twenties. The other was a burly dark-haired man of twenty-seven or twenty-eight. The older guy lost.

"Oh damn," he said, looking away from his colleague. He stepped forward, taking a scout knife from his pocket. He was tall, but he still had to reach to get hold of the rope. As he sawed at it, the dog's corpse twisted. Its paws brushed his chest. He curled his lip in disgust.

When the rope frayed, the younger officer came forward. He helped his older friend lower the beast to the ground. Tammany Bird stepped closer. He had a graceful, easy stride for such a big man. He stood above the animal, peering down at it.

"I'll be damned," he said. It was, again, nearly a whisper. He took a deep breath. He raised his heavy face to me. "How'd you come to find this?"

"Someone wanted me to find it," I said. I lit a cigarette. I turned my collar up. I had my overcoat on now against the chill. "Someone tapped on my window. Led me down here with a light."

"Male or female?"

"Not sure. Male, I think. Said he wanted to show me there was death in the woods."

He snorted. "Great. You figure it was a kid?"

"Maybe. Strange voice. Airy. Could've been a kid. He knew my name."

"Uh-huh. Sure. Suicides have him upset. Doesn't like you snooping around, writing about it."

He gave me a colorless glare. I tried to meet it. He shone his flashlight at me. I squinted, averted my gaze.

"You can't be surprised people know who you are, Mr. Wells," he said. "It's a small county." I raised my hand to my eyes. He lowered the light. "Can't say I'm all too thrilled about what you're doing either."

"All right," I said. "Don't be thrilled."

"Thank you kindly."

"Not at all."

He nodded. He looked off into the woods. I heard him mutter, "Not at all." Then he said to the officers: "Go get the blanket from the trunk, will you? No sense calling out E.M.S. for this." The two cops headed back up the slope toward the hotel. Bird watched them go. "Any idea which way this kid headed?" he said after a moment.

I shook my head. "Far as I could tell, he vanished."

That brought the colorless eyes of Chief Bird back around to me. "Vanished."

"Yeah."

"Huh. Well, I'm not surprised."

"You must run an entertaining county, then."

The eyes held me. They were like reef water: soft and clear on the surface, sharp and hard underneath. "Not usually," Bird said. "Usually, it's downright quiet. Nobody pays us any mind at all, then."

"Is that right," I said.

"Yeah. Yeah, that is right. Then suddenly, a little blood spills. That big tractor-trailer accident at the church last year. Triple murder a few years before that. Suddenly, why, every paper and TV station in the city wants to cover us. Interview the grieving, the way they do. 'What was your three-month-old son like before the truck ran over him, Mr. Creely?'" He shook his head. "Fact is, I was just getting ready to go to bed when I heard the dispatcher say your name on the radio. So I called up the boys, told 'em to swing by and pick me up. Know why?"

"Uh-uh."

"Wanted to see what kind of trouble you attract. I figured it'd be some kind. I just wanted to see what kind."

"Executed animals," I said. "I guess I'm the type." He kept glaring. I gave him glare for glare. "Lookit," I said, "just where do the decent folk of Grant Valley go wh... ...ney vanish into thin air after a good night of canine killing?"

A long, long moment passed in silence. Then Bird finally ended the staring contest, looked away. "Not much of a mystery, really." He pointed at the surrounding mist. "All these hills got limestone in 'em. All the limestone is full of caves. Whole network of caves up here. In one side of the hill, out the other, down to the bottom. Wouldn't be surprised at all to find a sinkhole somewhere right near by."

He swept the beam of his flashlight over the ground. It took him about seven seconds to find the place. No more than five feet from where we were standing, the ground dipped sharply. A little brooklet ran silently down from the hill into the dip. Bird's flashlight followed the path of the water. The light glinted off the surface, picked out the sheen of stones in the muddy bed. Then the water vanished. It went tumbling down a small round hole in the earth. The hole was just wide enough for a man to slip into.

Bird nodded. "Yeah. Figured."

"Could he be hiding down there?"

"He could be dancing down there for all I know."

"Think we ought to maybe drop in on him?"

"No," he drawled. "No thank you. No thank you at all. When I was a lad, now, I used to be able to find my way through these things like they were my own front yard. Knew just about every cave in the county. If I went down there today, the fellas'd have to call out the National Guard to find me. Some of 'em go on for miles." He shook his head. "Morning's soon enough. Wherever he was headed, he's half past there by now."

The officers returned with a blanket. They lay it on the ground next to the dog. They shifted the dog onto it. Bird sighed as he watched. "Okay. I guess we'll take this unfortunate creature back to the station, see what we can discover about its untimely demise." The blank eyes swept the area again.

"I'd like to see that report," I said.

He spared me a disdainful glance. "Public information," he said.

"That's right."

He heaved another sigh, a sigh as big as he was. "On the other hand, I don't need to tell you to keep away from this area until we come back in the morning."

"You don't need to tell me," I said.

"Good. That certainly puts my mind at rest. Just the thought of you having to find out what a hunkering piece of a son of a bitch I can be makes me bleed inside."

"I appreciate that."

"Good again. You have a pleasant evening, then, Mr. Wells."

I nodded. He turned. It was like watching an ocean liner swing around in the harbor. With a heavy breath he led the way back up the hill. The two officers followed. They carried the blanket between them with the dog rolled up inside.

I waited until their cruiser disappeared down the mountain. Then I went to my car to get a flashlight. I wanted to have a look at that cave.

10

I had only been in a cave once before, and that was to cover a disaster. It happened more than fifteen years ago, outside a little upstate town called Skyhawk. A guy by the name of Frank Nichols decided to take his nine-year-old son Gary and another boy spelunking. Old Frank was an advertising salesman for a radio station. He was one of those fellows who used to be good at things. He'd say, "Football? Oh yes, I used to be pretty good at football when I was a boy." The thing was, though, he'd never been any good at football. Never played. His mother made him sit on the sidelines. Frank used to watch the other kids go running past him, back and forth, and I guess he'd imagine he was one of them, and maybe that's what he remembered—the imagining. It was the same with tennis. His mother insisted he play tennis. She'd get him all dolled up in his whites and he'd go out there with the instructor and trip over his own feet for an hour. Then when he grew up, he'd say, "I used to be a fair hand at tennis when I was a boy." And that really was the way he remembered it.

Anyway, Frank used to be quite a spelunker in his youth. He'd never been in a cave, but clearly the talent was there. So one sunny weekend he gave these two boys the treat of a trip with the old master. Led them into a maze of caverns that would have baffled an expert. Two days later they were still there.

I did not mind going into that cave so much. I went down with a lot of cops and firemen, a lot of flashlights and torch helmets and ropes. Even in the tight spots I never felt any more underground than you do in a subway tunnel. The whole place was just as noisy and crowded.

I did get an idea, though: an idea of what it would be

like down there without the people, without the lights, without the noise. What it would be like to be down there alone in the heart of the earth where there is no fresh air or sun or sound of birds or signs of life. I got an idea of it when I looked into the faces of the children. They were in a chamber about a mile from the hole they'd entered. It was a big circular room with a flat rock floor and a low ceiling. Frank was sitting against the wall on one side of it, and he was long dead. A coronary. The two boys were huddled together on the opposite side. They'd spent about twenty-four hours with the corpse in the pitch dark. They were clutching each other, curled up in a single ball. One of them couldn't do anything but stare into space and drool and make a soft, high-pitched keening sound. For all I know, he's doing that still. The other kid, Gary, was dying. I helped haul his stretcher out to the light. He kept saying, "Tell my dad I wasn't afraid, okay? Tell him I wasn't scared at all." He went out about six hours afterward. No one made much of an effort to save him. I wrote his obit, though. I wrote about how he wasn't afraid. I told everybody.

It was from this experience that I'd formed my impression of what it was like to be in a cave alone. From the look in Gary's eyes. I remembered that look as I came down from the hotel parking lot, back into the woods, to the sinkhole.

I had a small flashlight with me now. Not much. One of those palm-size plastic ones. I keep it in the trunk for road emergencies. I made my way back to the oak where I'd found the dog. From there I spotted the dip in the earth again where it sat under the drifting mist. I took off my overcoat, laid it in the grass. I sat down on the rim of the sunken earth. I felt the leaves, damp and cold with the mist, chill the seat of my pants. I slid down slowly until my feet were in the tunnel. The water washed around my shoes. I stepped to the hole: a black circle in the ground, an eerie opening into the noth-ingness below. I got down on my knees. I put my face to the hole. I shined my flashlight into the blackness. I saw about two feet of green, slick stone. Then more blackness beyond.

I stuck one foot into the hole. I lowered myself in, turn-ing. I held on to the edge of the hole with both hands as my other leg went down. My feet sought purchase. I felt the rock sloping away beneath them. It was slippery with the brook water, but not particularly steep. I eased myself down until my head went into the hole. The night disappeared above me.

Slowly, my hands clutching at the wall, I sank down the slanting rock into the cave. It took about sixty seconds. A long sixty seconds. The rocks dug into my hands, my own weight strained my arms. The night rose up away from me, growing smaller, like a kite sailing into the sky. The still, thick air of the cave closed in around me, and the urge to climb back up tightened my throat. I breathed hard, fighting it off. The rock sloped gently for a few seconds more. Then it leveled out. I let go of the wall. I was standing under the earth.

Here, there was only the sound of the brooklet. There was only the light of the flashlight before me. Above me, framed in the small circle of the sinkhole, there was only the faint trace of the moonlit mist. The dark on every side of me, the dark that pressed against even the flashlight's beam, was so complete that it almost seemed solid. An impassable wall of dark.

I followed the water. I kept the flashlight trained on the ground, and edged along the thin stream as it continued to burble over the limestone. I lifted the beam now and then to study the place. It was an earthscape as barren as the moon. The walls, the floor, the ceiling of the cave: all of it was green and featureless, slick and wet. It was beautiful, but only the way the desert is beautiful, only the way the dead are sometimes beautiful if they died very young: it was beautiful in the monotony of its perfection. There was literally nothing here but rock and water. And dark. And me.

The path before me narrowed. I had to bend down. Then I had to drop to my knees. I felt the walls of the place move in until they were touching my shoulders. The ceiling grew lower until it was pressed against my back. I lay down. I stretched out. I was lying in the brook water. By the light of the flashlight I saw the little corridor open out in front of me. I dragged myself over the water and the stone.

At the corridor's end I climbed out carefully. There was a little drop-off. I sat on the edge for a moment, then lowered myself until my feet touched down.

I sent the beam dancing around me. It did not illuminate much. The dark overwhelmed it. But I did make out corridors to my left and to my right—openings into more darkness—I saw rugged walls leading high up to vaulting ceilings. I saw bats upside down in the far corners, their wings half scrolled around their curiously naked bodies. For a second I was struck by the fact that the sinkhole was no longer visible behind me. The earth above was no longer visible. I was sealed in. A baseball game could be going on up there in the night woods . . . a beautiful woman could be standing just above me with her skirt tapping against her legs in the breeze. . . . I could reach up to them, call out to them, and the world would continue on for them as it always had and they would come and they would go and they would never know I was here. The thought went through my head. And then the look in the eyes of Gary Nichols went through my head, and I felt my chest tighten. Then I lowered the flashlight's beam and saw the trail of the person who'd brought me here tonight.

It wasn't much. It was all in one corner, as if he or she had sat down to rest on the way here or back. I knelt down on the rock and played the flash over the remains. There was a plastic bag with what looked like bread crumbs in it; a couple of cigarette butts, Kents, that had been crushed out on the rock—I could see the smudge of the ash. There were some dead matches. And there was also, in a little pile, the charred remains of what looked like paper. I studied that closely, running my fingers over it gently. Whoever had burned it had taken care to crush the remains almost to nothing. But there was one corner of a piece that hadn't gone up completely. I could still make out the green of the page and its thick, grainy texture. I picked the fragment up and turned it over. There was nothing else to see. I replaced it with the other stuff to give Tammany Bird something to do in the morning.

I stood up. I cast the flashlight around the chamber one more time, eager to go.

"Don't forget, Mr. Wells," he said from beside me. "Death in the woods."

The high, light voice had come from one of the corridors. I whirled to find its source. But as I pivoted, a hand flashed out of the darkness. It struck me on the wrist. My hand went numb. The flashlight fell from my fingers. It tumbled through the air. The beam spun crazily once before me. Then the flashlight clattered on the rock. The light went out.

I stood stock still. The dark was shattering: so complete I felt entombed in it. *Tell Daddy I wasn't afraid at all.* My heart hammered in my ears. It was the only sound.

"Who are you?" I said—and I hated the sound of my voice. Hated the fear in it. "Who are you?" I shouted it this time.

"He did it. In the woods. He did."

The voice was moving away from me, its echoes fading down the corridor.

"He did it, did it, did it."

"What?" I shouted. "Killed her? Nancy? Who did what?"

"In the woods, Mr. Wells," said the echoing voice. "In the woods."

And then it was gone.

I knelt at once, passing my hand over the stone around my feet. I heard myself whispering. I whispered, "Come on, come on, come on . . ." My fingertips brushed the flashlight. I grabbed it. I felt for the switch. "Come on," I whispered.

The light went on. I turned—and now the beam was flashing and shaking everywhere. I turned and stuffed myself back into the little tunnel. I dragged myself through it quickly. I pulled myself out the other side, the brook water splashing around me. I looked up. I saw the moonlit mist through the sinkhole. I breathed with relief to see it.

Quickly, I followed that brook again, until the rock rose upward toward the night above. Then, my feet slipping under me, my fingers scrabbling over the stone, I struggled upward. My head emerged in the cool air. I sucked in a breath of that air—that fine, cold air. I pressed my palms against the earth and hauled myself up. Dragged myself out of the brooklet, out of the little cavity into which it ran. I climbed up onto the rim of the forest floor and tumbled down. I lay there, breathing hard, for a long moment.

Finally, I worked my way to my feet. I retrieved my coat, put it on. I walked slowly up the slope to the hotel and went back to my room. I let the door slip shut behind me. I took off my wet shirt and pants and collapsed, breathless, facedown on the bed.

I figured I was tired enough now to sleep without dreaming.

I was wrong.

11

Tammany Bird sent some men around in the morning. They went down into the cave with rope ladders and torch helmets and powerful flashlights. The smart way. After about a half hour they came up with the cigarettes and the matches and the paper. They informed me that the dog had apparently been poisoned before being hanged. Then they reiterated the official opinion that some kid, upset by the suicides, had decided to take it out on me. Then they drove away.

In the morning sunlight I tended to agree with them. In fact, the entire night—the dream, the chase through the woods, the dog, the cave—seemed to me now like one long continuous nightmare. It was breaking up, like ice on the spring water, the way nightmares do when morning comes.

Still, I tried to consider it. I tried to keep it together in my mind. As I sat in the parking lot, blowing the night chill out of the Artful Dodge, that voice came back to me under the revving engine. That weird, high, sexless voice: *Death*, he had said to me. *Death in the woods*. But Nancy Scofield had died in her room. Her parents had had to break the door down to get to her. The medical examiner had declared she died of an overdose of tranquilizers. Murder seemed pretty much out of the question. She hadn't even died in the woods. Not like the dog. Not like my daughter.

The old Dodge coughed and spat, and after a while, hummed quietly. I eased it out of the lot into the cul-de-sac before the hotel's front porch. I came around the curve and headed down the mountain.

Sure, I thought. It was a prank of some sort. A sick prank

by a sad and angry kid. The trick was not to let it get to me. In a way, that was the trick to the whole assignment.

I headed for town. On orders of my managing editor, I had to file as much of the series as I could before the weekend. I guess that way he could look at it personally and make sure I didn't try to sneak any serious journalism past him. So when I got to Main Street, I stopped off at the post office and sent the Scofield piece down to the city by express. After that I had breakfast in a nearby diner. I read the *Star*. I wanted to make sure Carey was mangling the Dellacroce trial as only he could. Then, satisfied, I went back to work.

The job now was Fred Summers. Sixteen. An old-fashioned kid, judging from his picture in the high school yearbook. Thin, long, gawky. Wore the school sweater. Very short blond hair. Big grin. Put a shotgun in that grin, he did, and pulled the trigger. Three weeks before.

Fred's father was Walter Summers. He had an engineering firm in Rogersville. He was also something of a local politician. He'd served five years on the Zoning Board of Appeals before he'd been elected, last November, to the county legislature. As I understood it, he was considered a good bet for county executive when the present man stepped down in two years.

Walter met me on his front lawn that morning. He had a ranch house in the Grant Valley woods. It was a twenty-acre spread that rose into the hills behind the house. Those hills were flaming with red oak leaves now, standing out from a background of yellow maples. As he extended his right hand to shake mine, Walter Summers gestured to the world around him with his left.

"Glorious autumn," he said as he shook my hand. He grinned, too, as he said it.

He was about my age, tall and muscular. He had ash-blond hair, thinning a little but not much. It capped a tan face of chiseled features. Piercing blue eyes surrounded by laugh wrinkles. An easy grin. He had the voice of a statesman and made it work. He spoke deeply, clearly, in round tones.

"My wife's inside. So's my son, my older son, Michael. He stayed home from school 'specially. We're all eager to talk to you. We think it could do a great deal of good for the community."

I nodded. Summers led me inside.

We entered a broad, well-lit living room. It was quite a place. It came complete with an eight-point stag's head mounted on the wall—a wall paneled with unfinished oak. The carpet was brown, and most of the furniture was one shade of tan or another. There were hunting and sports magazines on the coffee table and in the rack next to the easy chair. There was a pipe carousel on a little table, and ashtrays here and there. There was a fireplace, and on the mantle above it were photos of Walter Summers hunting or playing football. A football trophy was on one end of the mantle. A rifleman's trophy was on the other.

Mrs. Summers—Alice Summers—rose from the sofa as I came in: She was a small woman in her thirties. Still pretty, but she'd clearly been a real knockout once—movie-star quality, with her delicate nose and her full sensual lips and the auburn hair that rolled lush to her shoulders. Walter Summers stood looking at her proudly as she offered me her hand. And I couldn't help thinking—as my glance went from the stag's head to the football statue to Alice Summers—I couldn't help thinking: *This must be where he keeps his trophies.*

Mrs. Summers gave me a small, worried smile. Her eyes—green eyes—seemed worried too. It was the sort of look that seemed to be wondering whether you were going to be kind to her or knock her down. It was the sort of look that made you want to do one or the other. I smiled at her. Her eyes seemed almost to melt with gratitude, and at that moment, without knowing why, I knew I did not like Walter Summers.

We sat down.

"I guess the best place to start," Walter Summers announced, "is with what happened . . . I mean, what Fred decided to do. It came, as you might expect, as quite a shock." He paused for me to say, Yes, of course.

"Yes, of course," I said.

"Until that moment . . ." Summers went on, as if he were telling an adventure story at the Old Explorers Con-

vention. "This was in early October . . . and until the moment
it actually occurred, we had absolutely *no* idea that anything
was wrong. None." He glanced at his wife—for confirmation,
I expect. She stared down at the marriage rings on her fine,
small hands. She pursed her lips. She said nothing. Walter
barreled on. "Freddie was . . ." He pursed his lips, spread
his hands, considered. " . . . an average kid, I guess you'd
say. I don't know how else to put it to you. He liked girls
and sports and school. He always seemed cheerful. If he had
any problems . . . well, maybe he didn't apply himself enough
. . . to his grades, or maybe he could've done more in the
way of intramural activities. But those are average problems,
I think. Something that could happen to anyone. Teenagers,
you know." He sighed. He gazed at me earnestly. "Well,
anyway . . . one Saturday, last month, he went down to the
pond—the pond we have out in back. He took his hunting
rifle—a forty-forty shotgun—with him. I'd given it to him for
Christmas. After a while his older brother, Michael, went
down there and joined him. I was working at my desk upstairs.
I saw the two of them, chatting, sitting by the pond. They
were always pretty good buddies. Anyway, Michael got up
and started back to the house. His back was turned, but I
saw what happened next. Freddie was still sitting there by
the pond, facing away from me. But I saw him pick up the
shotgun from where it was on the ground beside him. I saw
him hold it in front of him. Then I heard the shot . . . and
I saw . . . well, you can imagine what I saw. He shot himself
in the head."

I glanced at Mrs. Summers. She was examining her hands.
Holding them together, turning them this way and that. She
seemed to see something in them, something far away. Her
lips trembled slightly.

Walter Summers sat back on the sofa. He looked up to
the right, over my head, like a man with a vision. Or a man
showing a reporter his best profile. He said: "I don't pretend
to understand it."

"Are you saying it might have been an accident?" I said.

He lowered his gaze to me at once. "Well, I . . ." He
smiled, sadly but wisely. "No. The medical examiner is a
good man. Charlie Ratzinger. He said suicide. But let me

put it to you this way: I'd like Charlie to come up with one good reason why an average Joe like Freddie—"

The phone rang. Mrs. Summers began to rise from the sofa. Her husband gestured to her.

"I'll get it," he said. "It's for me."

He cut a fine figure as he strode from the room. He went down the hall. I heard him pick up a phone. He said, "Hello?" Then the door closed behind him.

For a long, long minute, I sat there with Mrs. Summers. Mrs. Summers studied her hands with that distant trace of a smile. I shifted in my chair. I fiddled with my shirt pocket. Finally, I brought out a cigarette. I said: "Do you mind if I —"

"None of it's true, you know," she said. Her voice cracked. Her eyes, all at once, were swimming. She stared at her hands. "Not a word of it." She swallowed hard. "He couldn't . . . compete, Freddie. It wasn't . . . how he was. He couldn't . . . live up to . . . all of it . . . do you understand?" She gestured vaguely at the trophies around her.

I didn't say anything. I wanted to, but I didn't. I wanted to say: *Shut up, lady. I'm a reporter. Whatever you say, I'll put in the paper. And then whatever your husband does to you that makes you look so worried, he'll do again. Just shut up.* But I didn't say it. I didn't say anything. And maybe it didn't matter. Maybe she already knew. Maybe she just didn't give a damn anymore.

"You see, Freddie just wasn't *like* his father," she went on. "He kept trying, he tried so hard . . . and Walter . . . Walter just treated him like he was a failure, a disappointment. But it was just, it was just . . . Freddie was trying to do all the wrong things. He didn't belong on the football team. And hunting . . . he used to come back empty-handed. . . ." She laughed once, sharply. An unpleasant sound. "He thought he was a coward. . . . He thought . . . But he just wasn't the sort of boy who could shoot a deer. Once, after the three of them came back from a hunting trip, I found him lying on his bed and crying. Sobbing, literally, with his head in his arms. And do you know what he said to me, Mr. Wells? He said, 'Oh God, Mother. It was right in front of me, a perfect shot, and I threw a stone at it when they weren't looking. To scare it off, to make it run away before they shot it. It was so beautiful.' That's what he said. And then . . . and then he begged me not to tell. He begged me. And then the day he was cut from the football team . . ."

"Mrs. Summers," I began.

"Do you know he was positively brilliant at mathematics? Brilliant." She was leaning toward me now, her eyes urgently searching mine. "But he purposely didn't study because Walter—"

"Mrs. Summers, you have to understand that everything you say is on the record. I mean—"

"Print it!" Suddenly she was fierce. She pressed toward me even further. Her eyes blazed. Her voice roiled hoarsely deep in her throat. "Print all of it!" she said.

A door opened down the hall. At once she bowed her head and fell silent. In another moment Walter Summers came walking across the room with his vigorous stride. He clapped his hands together.

"Well," he said, "where were we?"

12

I stood by the pond in the backyard. The pond where Fred Summers had died. It was a small pool surrounded by little oaks and maples. Its clear water caught the reflection of the red and green and yellow leaves. The colors blended and spread out across the water's rippling surface. I smoked a cigarette and watched the gentle shifting of pastels. I thought of Mrs. Summers, and of her fierce, angry eyes.

In another moment I heard footsteps on the leaves behind me. I turned. There was Michael, a boy of about eighteen, coming from the house.

"They told me you'd be down here," he said. He held his hand out to me. I shook it. Michael had his father's grin. His father's muscular physique too—he wasn't thin as his brother had been. As for his face, it was, if anything, even more handsome than that of Walter Summers. His features were nearly perfect. His eyes were a more piercing shade of blue. The intensity of his gaze made you feel as if his attention were yours alone for as long as you wanted it.

"We can go back up to the house if you want," I said. It seemed like the thing to say.

"No," said Michael quietly. "I can stand it here. I wanted to talk to you alone."

I glanced back at the water. "You were with him—here—just before he died, weren't you?"

"That's right. I was."

"What did you talk about? That last time."

"He told me he was going to kill himself."

I let a lungful of smoke out slowly. I looked into Michael's so-blue eyes. His gaze never wavered.

"Why?" I said.

He sighed, his cheeks puffed. He put his hands in his pockets and leaned back until he was looking at the sky.

"That's hard to explain exactly. He talked about a sense of failure. That everything he did would turn out wrong. That everything I did would turn out right. He talked about our dad. Dad—jeeze—he's one of the greatest guys I know. He really is. But, maybe because of that, he's a tough image to live up to. I don't know. Maybe Fred tried too hard, and maybe Dad . . . well, Dad loved Fred, but he didn't know him. He expected him to be different than he was."

He spoke quietly, with simplicity and candor. When he was done, he gave a sad little shrug. The rest, he seemed to be saying, is beyond words.

I said, "You know, your father seems to think this happened without warning."

He smiled quietly. "You think he's trying to avoid a scandal, don't you?"

"I'm a reporter, son. I never think."

His shoulders lifted in a gentle laugh. "Well, I'll tell you. My father is going to be county executive here someday soon. Someday after that, he'll probably be a state senator. Maybe governor, I don't know. But he's also a father. And he was always a father first. He didn't always do the right thing, no. But he always had time for us. He was always there. So—maybe he *is* trying to avoid a scandal. But maybe concentrating on avoiding a scandal is his way of avoiding the pain. You might want to think about that."

"Fair enough," I said. "And what about you? What do you do for the pain?"

Again he sighed. His feet kicking the fallen leaves before them, he moved past me so that his back was toward me. He was at the pond's edge.

"You haven't asked me why I walked away," he said. I didn't answer. "He said, 'Mike, I wish I were dead.' He had the shotgun right there beside him. Right there. We talked for a long, long time. I told him to cheer up, that it wasn't so bad, it was all in his head. I told him there was plenty of stuff he was better at than me. Math. Jeeze, he was good at math. He said, you know, something like, 'Yeah, I guess so.'

And then I said, 'I'm going in to see what Mom's got for lunch. Come on.' And I walked away. I wasn't even at the house when the shot went off."

For a few seconds then he was silent. For a few seconds there was no sound but the deep blurt of the frogs at pondside. For a few seconds, I knew, he was reliving the moment when that shotgun went off. It was probably echoing in his head, fading in his head, exploding in his head again and again. Like the sound of a trapdoor.

Death, I thought suddenly. *Death in the woods.*

He turned around to face me. His eyes had lost some of their intensity, were clouded almost, as if he were turning that burning gaze inward now.

"You know, I can look in a person's eyes and see if he's ever grieved like I've grieved for Freddy," he said. "And if they have, you know what I do?"

I shook my head.

"I try to see how they handle it. How they live with this much hurting inside. Dad—he tries to pretend it's a political issue. Mom—she takes it out on Dad. Blames him for things he had no power over. The Scofields—have you talked to the Scofields?"

"Yeah."

"They join their support groups and all that." He paused. His gaze snapped clear suddenly. It was trained on me. "You work."

I didn't speak. I felt the heat of the cigarette against my fingers.

"You work, and you pretend you are your work," he said. "You make out you're some kind of walking question mark. No opinions, no desires . . ." He gestured at me. "No pain."

I dropped the cigarette on the autumn-hardened earth. I crushed it out with my foot. I took a good long time about it.

He was quite a kid. His father, strangely enough, was the pale imitation: False, where the son was sincere; facile, where the son was thoughtful. I had made up my mind about a lot of things when I'd taken a walk down to the pond. I'd made up my mind that Walter Summers was lying, that Alice Summers was telling the truth. A lot of that had changed in the few minutes I'd been talking to their surviving son. The things he'd said made sense to me. The way he'd said them rang true.

"So what about you?" I said, still looking down. "You still haven't told me how you—"

· He made a noise. A terrible noise. I glanced up. His face shook as he fought for control. His eyes were dry, but filled with pleading and desolation. In another instant the fit passed.

The boy took a few deep breaths. Then he said quietly: "Let's go inside."

I nodded. I followed him silently to the house. I had no other questions.

13

The Summers story wasn't an easy one to write.
I spent all Wednesday on the interviews, then
returned to my hotel room to batter it out. It
took the rest of the night. I pounded at the
typewriter hour after hour. I smoked cigarette after cigarette.
I sipped slowly at my glass of scotch. Every time I thought
I was finished, I'd glance longingly at the bed. Then I'd glance
from the bed to the page before me. And then I'd tear the
page out. Crumple it, toss it across the room at the waste-
basket. I'd watch it roll across the carpet. Then I'd start the
thing one more time.

I wanted, I guess, to get it from Michael's point of view.
To show that a kid's upbringing could be messed up, but that
maybe no one was to blame. To show the father's deceptions
as self-deceptions, the mother's rage as grief in disguise. I
wanted to show that some things can't be helped, even when
you do the best you can. That was the tack I wanted to take.
That struck me as the right tack. But it was hard to get it
down on the page.

I had drawn the curtains across the picture window. The
black slit where the curtains joined slowly grew violet. I
typed. The violet space turned blue. I saw the tendrils of
night mist fading under the cold morning sun. Finally, I rolled
the last page out of the machine. I stacked the piece together,
left it on the table, and went to bed.

When I woke up, it was too late to get the story down
to the office by mail, so I took the forty-five minute drive to
White Plains. The bureau there isn't much. Just a big second-
floor room above a furniture store. A few old wooden desks,

a lot of phones, two wire machines, and a couple of eager-looking kids trying to work their way south.

I retyped the story onto computer paper and fed it into the faxing machine. It rolled in slowly as the machine sent it down to the city over the phone wires.

I called the copy desk in New York. Alex answered.

"You get it?"

"Yeah, we got it. Looks good, Pops."

"Thanks, sonny-boy. Listen, is Lansing around?"

"Right here, Pops. Hold on."

Pops held on.

"Don't talk to me," Lansing said a second later. "I'm reading it."

"How's it look?"

"Ssh."

I lit a cigarette. Waited.

"Boy," she said softly then.

"Good?"

"Good."

"How'd Cambridge like the Scofield piece?"

"It was everything you could've hoped for."

"He get that puckered, mottled look he gets whenever I do something decent?"

"In spades."

"Just checking. What's the word around on the Della-croce trial?"

"Tell me you haven't been reading it."

"I wish I could."

"Did you see this morning's paper?"

"Yeah. Well, you can't do much with jury selection."

"The *Times* did."

"Uh-oh."

"Yeah." Lansing has a voice like a glass of red wine. It's rich and deep and smooth. It was even deeper now, but I couldn't tell if that was the sound of laughter or rage. "Dunlop over there had a piece on the fact that jurors in Manhattan federal court have been coming down with the flu in alarming numbers since the Dellacroce case started."

I cursed. "I told Carey to do that. I gave him the people

to call." I cursed again. "I even told him the *Times* was gonna run it."

"Ah, but Carey had a better idea."

I tried to imagine Carey having an idea. I didn't get very far. I could see his fat, sweaty face straining behind his pencil moustache. I could see his cheap tie bobbing with the motion of his double chin. I could even see his tan polyester suit getting damp under the armpits. After that the mind boggled.

"I'm afraid to ask," I said.

"He did a history of the courthouse."

I laughed, more or less. "If the mob has a medal, Cambridge'll get it for this."

"Even he couldn't run it. In fact . . ." She paused. I pictured her glancing over her shoulder to see who was listening. She spoke softly: "In fact, keep your guard up, okay? He's been gunning for you for a long time. Now he's made himself look bad doing it, and he's really on the warpath. And this place wouldn't be any fun without you."

"Sure it would. Lots of places are."

"No place I've been."

I let that pass. "Say, what's he got against me anyway? Just because I'm not relatable enough . . ."

"It's not that. You know it's not that." Another pause.

"Yeah?" I said.

"It's who you are. And who he's not."

"Mm. I guess I can't help him there."

She didn't say anything. I took a long drag on my cigarette. She didn't say anything some more.

"Come on, Lansing," I said. "What's up?"

"You didn't have to do it this way, you know," she said.

"What way?"

"You know. The profiles. The kids. The parents."

"That's my angle. Don't you like it?"

"You don't have to show Cambridge you can take it. He knows you're a tough guy."

Now I was silent. I let her hear the hiss as I blew smoke into the handset.

"Don't push yourself too far, John," Lansing said. "You've got a right to be human."

"Yeah, but why change now?"

"I'm serious, Wells."

I thought it over. "I'm almost done, Lancer. I got one more to do. Michelle Thayer. If I can finish the interviews by tomorrow, I'll come back and write the rest from there."

There was a pause. "It'll be good to see you," she said.

"Don't talk to me like that, Lansing."

"Shut up."

"Bye."

"Bye."

As I drove back up to Grant Valley, heading toward the Thayer place, I didn't think about what Lansing said. I thought about Michelle. The last profile. When I was done with her, I'd do a facts-and-figures piece, and some kind of wrap-up. The easy part.

But I still had to get through this one. And this one was going to be tough.

She'd died ten days ago, no more. I hadn't even thought her mother would speak to me. But when I called—and man, I hated making that call—she didn't hesitate for a minute.

"You want to do a story about my daughter?" she said softly. "Come on, then. I'll give you a story." Her name was Janet. She was divorced.

Her daughter Michelle had been a straight-A student. Her daughter had been fifteen. Her daughter had walked into the woods behind her house one mild fall evening. She'd climbed up an oak tree and sat on a branch. She had a rope with her. She tied one end of the rope around the branch and the other around her neck. Then she jumped. So, yeah, I drove to the Thayer house thinking about Michelle.

The way went through town, past the high school and onto the highway beyond. For a mile or so the going was easy. But when I hit the first exit, I turned off. I made another quick turn, and I was in the woods again, on a rutted road that twisted underneath my tires like it was trying to get away.

It was a grim day. Big dark clouds had rolled over the sky on a wind with a touch of winter in it. On every side of me the forest pressed in, gray and gloomy. I noticed as I drove—as I drove and thought about Michelle—I noticed there were more For Sale signs here than on the other side of town. There were fewer bulldozers hiding away in the trees. I guessed this was not prime real estate. The few houses I saw bore that out. They were shabby, small, gray as the sky. There were some with small front yards that were piled high with car parts and busted-up furniture and garbage. There were trailers that seemed to have been parked behind the nearest tree and forgotten. There was even a moldering, abandoned schoolhouse of some sort, its clapboards rotting, caving in, its windows black and broken.

The Thayer house wasn't much, but it made the effort. It was a small frame place with a little porch. It needed a coat of paint, all right, but there were pretty gingham curtains in the windows, and the little lawn that had been cleared out of the surrounding forest was cropped and tended.

I first saw it from about two hundred yards away as I crested a winding hill above it. Mrs. Thayer had described it to me over the phone, and I knew it was the right place. The sight of it made my stomach turn over. I felt a cold sweat break out behind my ears. I thought about Michelle.

A straight-A student. Like my daughter was. Fifteen years old. Olivia was too. She'd hanged herself in her backyard woods. That was close enough. Too close. I looked at the Thayer house and my lips felt dry. I glanced to the side, toward the autumn trees falling away below me.

And I saw Death in the woods.

There was some kind of a wall out there. A stone wall, the kind you see in second-growth forests that were farmlands in the old days. For one instant I could have sworn I saw him standing just behind it: a macabre figure, half blending into the gray background, half standing out against the yellow leaves. A man—or something like a man—dressed all in black. But where his head should have been there was nothing but a skull, an eyeless skull with the empty sockets staring straight at me.

I took a sharp jolt as the front right tire of the Artful Dodge grabbed hold of the road's shoulder. I wrestled with the wheel, fighting to bring the car back onto the pavement. The tire fought back for a few feet, then surrendered. I hit the brake. The car eased to a stop.

I got out. I looked over the Dodge's roof. Slowly, I scanned the forest before me. My eyes flicked from tree to tree. He was gone.

Now, finally, Lansing's words returned to me. I heard her voice again: *Don't push yourself too far, John. You've got a right to be human.*

And I heard that other voice too. That weird, high, light, almost inhuman voice that had come to me out of the fog as if out of my own nightmares.

There's death in the woods, Mr. Wells. Death in the woods.

14

"You look a little pale, Mr. Wells. Are you all right?"

Janet Thayer stood in the foyer. She was still holding the screen door in her hand. I'd just come in off the porch. I had my hands in my pockets and was glancing around casually, pretending I was fine.

"Yeah, I'm fine," I said quickly. I was annoyed with myself. *Don't push yourself too far. Pops.* "I just . . . I just ran my car off the road, shook myself up, that's all."

"Oh. Can I get you a glass of water?"

"Thanks."

She went before me into the kitchen. It was a room run ragged, the yellow floor tiling brown and lumpy, the yellow walls peeling and stained. She ran the faucet into a rusty sink.

"I'm a nurse," she said. "My friends tell me I'm always on about somebody looking too this or too that. I started on you fast. You hardly had a chance to say hello."

She handed me a glass of water.

"Hello," I said.

"Hi."

She was short and substantial. Not fat, just sturdy. Her hair was dyed blond. It was frizzy and unkempt. Her face was round and well worn, but I pegged her at under forty. Just worn is all. She was dressed in a rumpled pink blouse and jeans. At first glance she didn't look like a woman in mourning. But that was only at first glance. Then I looked in her eyes—they were pale green eyes with flecks of gold in them. They were hard, steely eyes that had seen a lot of the bad old things in a bad old world. They'd cried plenty, all right, but they weren't about to do it in front of me.

She had a pack of cigarettes in a teddy bear cookie jar on the counter. She took one and offered one to me. She leaned against the counter's edge while I lit us up.

"Well," she said. "You look like a reporter."

"It's the overcoat."

She snorted smoke out through her nose. "This the assignment of your choice?"

"Not exactly."

She shrugged. "Some of them like it. I watch them on the television. They go out and grab some mother whose three little kids just burned up in a fire, or they interview some cop's wife after he's just been blown away. I can see it: it's how they get their kicks."

"Not me. I drink."

"So do I. Now."

She kept her eyes on me. She had something to say, but she wasn't sure yet if I was the one she wanted to say it to. All I knew was: she was not the sort of woman to try to fool. I lifted my cigarette, ran my thumb thoughtfully over my lip.

"I used to like it well enough, I guess," I said. "I used to get a charge out of being on the scene of a fire when the women jumped with their babies in their arms . . . or watching the cops tell jokes and smoke cigarettes over the body of a murder victim until the M.E. showed. I used to like to tell people I'd seen those things. I talked out of the side of my mouth when I told them. I thought it was just the thing."

"So now you cover church socials."

"Mostly I cover the courts. Mostly nowadays I like to watch bad guys get put away. I like to wave at them as they go."

She smiled. Smoke seeped out from between her teeth. She tossed her cigarette back into the full dishpan. The butt hissed and died. She pushed off the counter.

"Follow me," she said.

I tossed my cigarette after hers.

We went back through the foyer. Through a small living room with a picture window on the road. I got a glimpse of old stuffed chairs under standing lamps. I got a sense of disorder. Then we were moving up the stairs. They groaned beneath my feet as we rose.

We went down a gray and dusty hall. We passed her bedroom first. I saw a double bed, a lot of old lace, stained and ragged at the edge. There was a photograph on the bed table. I saw it briefly as we passed by. Michelle had had a pretty smile.

There was a door to the right—the bathroom—and one more door on the left down the hall. That door was closed. Janet Thayer took a key from the pocket of her jeans and stuck it in the old-fashioned keyhole under the knob.

"I keep it locked," she said. "I don't know why." She looked up at me. "To keep it all in there, I guess."

I nodded.

The door opened. She led the way inside.

Everything was different here. There was no dust, no stains, no wear. It was a clean, pink room with a large canopied bed in the middle of it. There was a pink quilt on the bed, and large lacy bolsters. The walls were spotless. They were yellow. The paint was fairly new. There were stuffed animals here and there, and school books and a vanity table with a mirror. There were snapshots tucked up under the mirror. I walked over and took a look.

Michelle had had a tender face, delicate and sweet. She was short like her mother, but her figure was slender and gently curved. I saw her in one photo, standing in a party dress, looking uncomfortable with her hands folded before her. She had shiny brown hair down to her shoulders. She had a round dimpled face with small features. She was looking into the camera with a gaze that seemed at once shy and direct. I was held for a long moment by the expression in her eyes, an expression full of both pity and laughter. It was a woman's gaze in a girl's face.

I turned away.

"She was lovely," Janet Thayer said.

"Yes."

"But I guess I would think that."

"No, it's true."

Now, for just a moment, I saw the look in her eyes that I was expecting: the agony I'd seen in the Scofields' eyes, and the Summerses'. But it was deep down under the hard green, and it appeared only for an instant, and sank away again.

"She could draw." She gestured to a bureau on the opposite wall. There was an artist's pad on top of it. I went to it, opened it. "She used to draw all kinds of funny pictures of me. Dress me up in different costumes, give me a moustache. It gave her a real kick."

I leafed through the pad. The light green pages wafted down in front of me. There were sketches of Mrs. Thayer. Of the woods. Of dogs and cats and flowers. There were sketches of some of the kids from the high school.

I stopped. I had come to a self-portrait. Michelle Thayer in Michelle Thayer's hand. It was a picture of a girl on the very cusp of womanhood. A girl full of the energy of that moment. Smiling brightly—beaming even—her cheeks high, her eyes bright.

I glanced up at Mrs. Thayer. Suddenly, what I saw in her eyes was neither toughness nor pain. It was something hot and ferocious. Something almost mad. She was nodding at me. She kept nodding and nodding. Her mouth was taut and grim and damp at the corner. This—this self-portrait— was what she had wanted me to see.

"Look at it, Mr. Wells," she said. It came in a whisper. The kind of whisper you hear in sanitorium halls. "Look at it. She drew that a week before she died. Look at it good."

Slowly, I turned back to the picture. But all I could see now was the color of the paper: that light green on the roughly textured page. The same color, the same texture, as the corner of paper I had found under the earth in the limestone cave.

"That's not the face of a girl who killed herself," Janet Thayer said.

Again I looked up at her.

"My daughter was murdered," she said.

15

It was Friday night. It was late. I was back in
the city room of the *Star*. An eerily quiet place
these days. Once, not too long ago, it was filled
with the clatter of wire machines and the bells
of typewriters and the shouts of reporters from one desk to
another. There were copyboys carrying long sheets of the wire
news and laying them beside each writer, murmuring "urgent"
or "bulletin" or nothing at all as they went past. There was
the sound of editors cursing.

All that was gone. You could see the top of your neigh-
bor's head over the little walls of the cubbyholes, but no one
looked up much. The keys of the computer terminals hardly
made any sound at all. The wire machines were built right
into the things. You could press a button and call the local
wire up onto your monitor, or the A wire or the sports or the
weather or business. When something important happened,
a polite sort of boop went off, and up in the right-hand corner
of your screen, above the copy, a word or two appeared:
Urgent, Bulletin, Late Stocks, whatever. Then you pressed
the HOT button and the story came up in front of you. All
very neat, all very clean. When you finished your story, the
editor could call it up on his screen and mangle it without
saying a word. And if you wanted to express your opinion,
you didn't even have to shout anymore. You could just send
a message from one keyboard to another. Then the editor got
the "message" signal on his screen and he pressed a button
and the words, "[From Wells] You suck, you illiterate scum!"
appeared right before him. Or something very much like.
There was no paper, no mess, no muss, no fuss. Even the
printers were covered with glass to muffle the noise from them.

So I was tucked neatly into my cubbyhole, hunched before my Olympia, hacking away under the fluorescent lights. An island of sound in the surrounding silence. I was finishing my story on Michelle Thayer.

When it was done, I gathered the pages together. I sat back in my chair and lit up a cigarette. I read the first 'graph over through the smoke.

Lansing came in. I saw her across the top of the page. She strode from the front doors to the city desk. She was wearing a long orange coat. It was open, and the two halves of it fluttered out as she walked. She had a camera strapped around her neck. Her purse was in her hand.

It made me smile to see her like that. It made me think of the first time we'd met, about a year, a year and a half before. She was a stringer then. A bona fide journalism-school graduate, trying to bust on to the staff. She kept a police radio in her car, and every time some store clerk got blown away somewhere, she'd rush over to the scene and try to file it with us.

Then one fine summer's day a young man who worked in his parents' upper-east-side funeral home went berserk with a fire axe. Killed his father, his mother, and his sister, then went to work on the corpses being readied for burial. This amused one of my editors, so a photographer named Rich Gruber and I ambled over there. We arrived before the cops had finished cleaning up the place. A detective friend of mine pointed me to a rear entrance and told me to stay out of sight.

Gruber and I snuck inside for some exclusive pictures. We were in a long corridor. Red carpet on the floor, yellow lamps on the ceiling. Eerie. It led down to the room where the cops were trying to figure out which body part went with which. We started toward the room.

We'd taken about three steps when the door behind us cracked open again. In walked this long blonde with two cameras hanging around her neck.

Gruber and I were shaken. We weren't supposed to be in there and we knew it.

The blonde looked us over. She said, "All right, you

two. Get the hell out of here. The police can take their own goddamned pictures."

Gruber started for the door.

"And you," she barked at me.

I started to follow Gruber. Then I got a closer look at her eyes. Uncertain eyes. I stopped. I was standing right in front of her. "Nah," I said. "Almost, sister. But not quite."

Gruber's mouth fell open. "What do you mean? You mean she's one of us?" He was beside himself. "Oh baby. Oh man. Let's kick her the hell out of here, pal. Even the cops'll back us."

"I've got as much right to be here as you do," she said.

"Yeah. None."

"All right, lady." I poked my finger at her. "Who're you with?"

"The *Star*." She faltered a little. "Freelance, anyway."

I laughed. "Oh yeah. You're the one with the radio. And the dead store clerks. What's-her-name. Lansing."

"That's right. And take your goddamned finger out of my face. Who the hell do you think you are?"

I told her.

She was pretty even when she went pale. "Damn it," she said.

I thought it over for a minute. I'd seen her stuff. It wasn't bad. I said, "Come on, Richie. I'll buy you breakfast."

Gruber nearly shouted, which would have had the real cops down on us for certain. "Are you joking, man? This is the centerfold tomorrow."

As it turned out, he was right. It was the centerfold. And a month later Lansing was on staff.

Now she was bent over talking to Mark Parrish, the night city man. I watched her. Telling him what she had, pushing for her angle. He nodded. When she straightened, she caught me looking at her. She smiled and came over.

"You're back." She took her coat off, dumped it on a chair. She hiked herself up to sit on my desk. She was wearing a skirt tonight. She swung her legs in front of me. I watched her legs.

"Where you been?" I asked her.

"Gracie. The mayor's limo hit a cab."

"Oh jeeze. Is he hurt?"

"Don't be silly. Only a silver bullet can stop him."

"I'll pass that information on to the right people."

She nodded at my story. "Is that the end of it?"

I tossed the pages onto the Olympia. "Of the profiles, anyway. I'll do the summary next week for Sunday." I reached for the ashtray, jabbed out the 'rette. I rubbed my eyes with both hands. I was beat.

"Well?" said Lansing. "Is it good?"

"Read it."

She gave the story a speculative glance. Then she gave one to me. "Tell it," she said.

I met her gaze for gaze. "Give it a rest, kid."

"Go on. Live a little. Tell it, Wells."

I sighed. I sat silent a while. The effort to tell it seemed like a big one. Finally I said: "All right. Michelle Thayer. She was sweet. She was shy. Gentle. Good-looking. She liked baby-sitting and going out for sodas with her friends."

"Boys?"

"So-so. A little bit slow with boys, I guess." I was thinking it over now. Staring across the room where the night people drifted ghostly through the cubicle maze. The office, lit by the fluorescents, seemed oddly bright, oddly quiet. You could sense the city darkness hovering at the windows. "Her mother—Janet—married an Army guy," I said. "He dumped her about two months later. About seven months later Michelle was born. Gave Mrs. Thayer a sort of jaded view of the male sex in general."

"So she treated her daughter to a lot of lectures about the dangers of men," Lansing said.

"That's it."

"Not so good."

"I guess." I pulled another cigarette from the pack. Toyed with it, unlit, between my fingers. "All in all, I got the feeling Mrs. Thayer kept a tight rein on the girl. She told me Michelle didn't seem to mind it. . . ."

"You interview Michelle's friends?"

"Friends. Teachers. The cops. She had a lot of friends. She was the kind of girl the other kids went to for advice.

Good listener. Slow to judge. Never told anyone her own problems. Some of her friends said her mother used to confide in her, kind of like their roles were reversed." I glanced up at Lansing. She was watching me closely. Her expression was serious, intent. "The psychologists tell me you have to look for that with teen suicides. The kid who has to play parent. Has to be perfect. Can't ever complain."

"Like Richard Corey in the poem," Lansing said. "Everyone admires him, looks up to him. One day, he goes off and blows his brains out."

"Yeah. Well. Yes and no. There were clues in her case. I guess there are always clues." I closed my eyes, pinched the bridge of my nose between my fingers. "God, I'm beat. I don't know why I'm so beat. Long day I guess."

Lansing studied me. Said nothing.

I went on. "Her friends said she'd started to get secretive. Stopped going out for sodas. Started to disappear after school."

"She wasn't going home?"

I shook my head. "She told her mother she was working on a special project with her art teacher. She wasn't. Mrs. Thayer still won't believe she was lying. Says there's some mix-up . . ."

I rooted in my shirt pocket for a match. Tugged it out. Lit up. I smoked hard, fogging myself in.

"You ever find out where she went? After school?"

"No." I waved the cigarette. "Could've been anywhere. Maybe a boyfriend. That makes sense. Maybe she just wanted to get away from her mother."

"Drugs?"

"No. At least not in the autopsy."

"Okay. So?"

"Yeah. So. So the mother says her daughter was murdered." I glanced up. Lansing's expression hadn't changed. "You don't seem surprised."

"Are you?"

I heard myself sigh again, more deeply now. I didn't answer her. "I tried to write it straight. I gave the facts. She hanged herself. In the woods. In her backyard."

Lansing closed her eyes. The corners of her mouth turned down. "Go on," she said.

"Then, third 'graph or so, I quoted the mother saying her kid was murdered. And I told what she looked like when she said it. Wild. Hot. Almost mad. Then I quoted Tammany Bird—he's the county police chief—good man. I quoted him saying a thorough investigation had been done and he was convinced it was suicide. Then I had the kids talking about how her personality had changed and how she'd started to go off by herself and everything. Tagged it with my expert, a psychologist, Dr. Cartwright. She talked about . . ." I took a long drag off the butt. I watched the rim of its paper wrinkle with flame, turn to gray ash. "She talked about guilt. How a mother—a parent—might find the idea of murder more comforting than suicide." I blew out the last of the smoke. "That was it."

Lansing spoke softly. "Sounds like a good story."

I nodded. "It is a good story." I gestured at the pages on the typewriter. "But it's not the whole story."

Then I told her. I told her about the forest and the body of the dog. The dog hanged from a tree, as Michelle had been. I told her about the figure who had vanished into the caves beneath the mountain. About the weird, airy voice that had spoken to me out of the dark. *He did it. Death. Death in the woods.* I told her about that too: about the figure of Death I'd seen standing outside the Thayer house.

"None of that's in there," I said. "I didn't write a word of it."

"Okay. Why not?"

"Because I found a piece of paper down in the cave. It was just like the paper on Michelle Thayer's drawing pad. The only thing I can figure is that Mrs. Thayer—or maybe someone who knows her, boyfriend, colleague, someone who's gotten caught up in her way of seeing things—I figure maybe they heard I was in town and decided to put on a show. Convince me Michelle didn't kill herself. That she was murdered. And I guess I figure Janet Thayer doesn't need that published in our daily history of the world for all to see. At this point it just doesn't seem to matter very much."

Lansing lifted her shoulders, shivered. "Hanging a dog. Running around in a death mask. That's a long way to go to convince you."

I crushed out the cigarette. Reached for another. I fiddled with it between my fingers. "Is it?" I said.

"Why would they take so much trouble?"

"Oh, knock it off, Lansing," I said sharply. "You know why."

She bit her lip, looked away from me. She looked at her legs as they swung back and forth over the edge of the table. Nice legs. "Yeah," she said quietly. "I know why. Because you can solve a murder. You can catch someone. The cops come and take him away. Send him to court. Send him to jail. Not like a suicide. You can try to solve that forever." And she raised her eyes. "Is that pretty close?"

I grunted. Snatched the Thayer story off the typewriter and pushed out of my chair. "Anyone ever tell you you suffer too much?" I said.

"My mother. Every Sunday. Let me write up the mayor and I'll buy you a drink."

"No thanks."

"Okay. You buy."

"I'm going home."

"You want a medal?"

"I want some sleep."

I walked past her. Wove around the walls to the city desk. Dumped the pages in front of Parrish.

He looked up from his computer terminal. "What's this?"

"My application for sainthood," I said, on my way to the door. "Call me when it's approved."

16

SUICIDE MOM: IT WAS MURDER.

That was the banner on Sunday's paper. That was the first in our series on teenage suicide. That was relatable. That was Cambridge. No one else could have done it.

I got the paper at the stand outside my building. I stripped the funnies off and dumped them in the trash. I was at the corner of Eighty-fifth and Third when I saw the headline.

From then on I carried the paper gingerly, as if it were a bomb that might go off. I took it to the Athens coffee shop. I sat at the counter. I ordered a bagel and a black coffee. I sat on the stool with my hands folded in front of me. The *Star* lay closed beneath my hands. I stared at it.

I ate the bagel. I drank the coffee. I got a refill. I lit a cig. I opened the paper to page three.

GRANT VALLEY MYSTERY, was the head over my byline. " 'Somebody killed my daughter!' Janet Thayer sobbed." That was the lead.

I read the rest. It was Cambridge all right. The prose was unmistakable. It was like a garrote victim who hadn't quite been finished off: It squealed and wheezed. The dry-eyed, enraged, half-crazy Janet Thayer whom I had interviewed was gone. In her place was a grieving mother overwhelmed at her weakest moment by a justice system she never made. Tammany Bird was not a shrewd, imposing officer of the law anymore. He was a hick cop now, caught in a clumsy cover-up, ready to enforce his version of the truth at all costs. Rod Steiger could have played him in the picture.

The psychologist was gone. And as for Michelle's fellow students . . . Cambridge led into their comments with: "To the kids who knew her, an atmosphere of mystery and fear hung over Michelle in her final days." Then he cut their quotes to nothing to make it stick.

I smoked my cigarette. I drank my coffee. I turned to the jump page. I read to the end. Impressive: He'd gotten through the entire thing without using the phrase "Death Orgy," one of his favorites. I crushed out my cigarette in an ashtray. I crushed it out slowly. I twisted it around as I crushed it out. I paid the waitress, left a tip. I took the paper out into the street and gave the front page to a woman who was walking her dog. We have strict sanitation laws in New York City.

It was a long Sunday. I called the paper. Ray Marshall was on the desk for the weekend. Cambridge was not there. He and his wife and their daughter had gone out to Long Island to visit the grandparents. Nice.

"He was in yesterday, wasn't he?" I asked.

"Yeah," said Marshall. There was a pause. "He came in specially."

"What a guy."

"Sorry, Wells."

"Thanks, pal," I said. Ray was one of the good ones. He'd been a decent reporter before they promoted him. Knew how to talk you through a shoot-out, supply you with cool when yours was gone. He had nothing to prove, so he could leave good copy alone. He didn't have to tell me he'd tried his best on this one.

I went to a movie. It was about a cop who shoots people in the face if he suspects them of anything. I liked it. I came out and had lunch. I went to another movie. It was about a guy with a butcher knife who stabs an entire county to death one person at a time. I liked that too. I came out and went to the launderette. I did my laundry. I read the sports section. The sports section in the *Times*. I went home and watched TV. I went to bed and watched the clock. Monday came. I went out to breakfast. I read the *Star*. They'd run the Scofield piece as a follow-up to Thayer. Other cases that might need reopening. That sort of thing. I waited until ten o'clock. Then I went in to kill Cambridge.

The office of the *Star* is on Vanderbilt Avenue, right across the street from Grand Central Station. I took the subway. I was there by ten-fifteen.

I went past security to the elevator. I rode the elevator to the twelfth floor. I went through the glass doors into the city room. I went toward Cambridge's office. The door was closed.

Lansing and McKay had been talking by the far wall. Lansing was leaning against the wall. McKay stood before her, drinking a cup of coffee. Out of the corner of my eye I saw Lansing's head come up when I walked in. I kept walking toward Cambridge's door.

She was fast. She got there before me. She stood in front of me and put her hands on my shoulders. I could smell her. She smelled good.

"Get out of my way, Lansing," I said.

"Wells—"

"I'm going to kill him. It's the best thing for everyone. Trust me on this."

"Wells—"

"Really, Lansing. Get out of my way."

"Stop him, McKay."

McKay was standing beside me now. "Wells—" he said.

"It's no good saying 'Wells.' "

"John—"

"No , that's no good either. The future of the journalistic profession is on the line."

Lansing's arms were straining against me now. She had to brace her feet to make a stand.

"Oh Jesus," she said. "He's really going in there."

"Wells," McKay hissed, "he'll fire you."

I turned to him, stunned. "McKay," I said, "I'm going to kill him. They'll put me in prison. I won't need a job."

The office door opened. Cambridge peeked his head out. Lansing let me go.

"What's going—" He pretended to notice me and be surprised. "Johnny! Hey there, buddy. Great series." He wiggled his hand back and forth in the air. "Had to doctor it up a little bit, you know. Make it relatable. But . . . the basics were really there. No mistaking it. You do the finish-up pieces, then we'll put you right back on Dellacroce. Carey can't wait to get off it." He grinned.

I grinned. "I'd like to speak to you, Bob," I said.

"Oh gee," he said, glancing at his watch. "I'd like to, but you know, I got to go up and meet with . . ." He gestured upward with his thumb. ". . . the people upstairs."

"This won't take long," I said. How long can a man keep breathing when you're standing on his throat? "We can talk in your office, or right here."

He stopped smiling. He glanced at Lansing. He didn't want her to hear this. "Hey, sure, I can spare a few minutes. What the hell?"

He went into his office. I smiled at Lansing. "Call the police," I said. She covered her face with her hand. I followed Cambridge in and shut the door behind me.

Cambridge sat behind his desk. He raised his hand. "Now, Johnny, I know you're upset—"

"Let me explain something, Bobby," I said. "Fuck you."

"Hey. Hey, hey, hey," said Bob.

"Fuck you, and the relatable horse you rode in on."

"Hey. Really. I'm serious," he opined.

"You butchered my story."

"I didn't butch—"

"You butchered my story, and you wrote things under my byline that weren't true."

"Now, just, just, let's calm down here."

Which was when I started screaming. What I screamed was: "Calm down? That was a little girl who died, you stupid son of a bitch!"

Cambridge had no choice. He stood up and started screaming back. "This is always what I get from you, Wells! I get bullshit! That's all I get!"

We stood on opposite sides of the desk. We each pointed a hand at the other. We screamed.

"Those are real people—" I screamed.

"Bullshit and . . . and opposition," he screamed.

"You can't just turn them into characters in your relatable fairy tale—"

"You've just tried to stand in my way—"

"That woman's half-crazy with grief! You make her sound like Sherlock Holmes, for Christ's sake!"

"The times change, Wells, that's what you can't stand!"

"You libel the goddamned police chief!"

"That's what you can't stand! Times fucking change!"

"You cry cover-up— Oh, fuck you, times change."

"Don't tell me . . . Fuck you too!"

"Fuck you, Cambridge!"

"Oh yeah?"

"Yeah. Fucking yeah." I waved my hand at him in disgust and started for the door.

"It's a shame what's happened to you, Wells," he called after me. "You used to be one of the greats."

I stopped. I blinked. I turned around. Cambridge turned pale under his tan. *It's November*, I thought. *Where does he get a tan?* I walked slowly back to his desk.

"Let me tell you what's going to happen now," I said.

He put his hands on his hips. "Okay. Okay, you tell me."

I took a breath. "In about three weeks this city is going to blow sky-high. The transit chief is just the beginning. There's a witness coming up at the Dellacroce trial who's going to implicate enough officials to make a whole new division of government."

Cambridge backed up a little. "You have that solid?"

"I practically have it written."

"What? Like . . . City Hall?"

"Maybe Albany, buddy."

"Oh shit."

"Oh shit is right. And let me tell you what else. Everytime there's a big development, it's going to be in the *Daily News* one full day before it hits the *Star*. One full day, Cambridge. And you know why? Because I'm going to be working for them. Go and explain that to the . . ." I jabbed my thumb at the ceiling. ". . . the people upstairs."

His face went blank. "Oh hey, now wait a minute."

I waved my hand at him again. I started for the door again. "Go to hell," I said. I had my hand on the knob.

"Wait. Really, Wells, wait."

I stopped again. I turned again. "I want you off my copy."

He lifted his shoulders. "Hey, I was only trying—"

"Off my fucking copy."

"Okay. Sure. Fine."

"And I want the rest of the suicide story killed."

"Uh-huh. Uh . . . okay."

"Now, whatever your little relatable projects are, I won't stand in your way—"

"Good."

"But the courts belong to me."

He nodded slowly.

"The courts are mine, Cambridge."

"All right. The criminal—"

"Right. And one more thing."

"I know, I know. You want back on the Dellacroce case."

"I want back on the Thayer case."

His mouth actually dropped open. "What?"

"I'm gonna check it out from top to bottom. If she was murdered, then I won't look like an idiot. If it was suicide, I want a page three retraction including the fact that the story wasn't mine."

"Oh, come on, Wells."

"Go ahead," I said. "Go upstairs. Discuss it with the people. Ask Mr. Sandler if he wants me at the *News*. Or Bush."

"Johnny—"

"Meanwhile, I'll pack for Grant County."

17

I went home that night and drank. Did I drink? I drank, all right. I sat with a bottle while the sun went down; I went down with it under an amber haze of J & B.

The shadows gathered. That's what shadows do at dusk, they gather. Most of them, I think, gather in my apartment. It's a good place for shadows. A big one-bedroom that almost looks abandoned. There are no pictures on the wall, and the paint is chipping. The dust has collected in large snowy balls under what furniture there is: a bed, an old dresser, a table, a couple of chairs. There's a TV stand with a TV on it. There's a rickety old desk, too, with a rickety old typewriter on it. None of it gives the place much life. The living room's two windows open on Eighty-sixth Street: The glaring light of movie-theater marquees keeps one wall well lit all night long. Right across from me, at the triplex, they were playing a picture about monsters, one about spaceships, and one about Kung Fu. I could read the marquee as I sat at the desk with my bottle and my glass and my pitcher full of melting ice. I could see the city growing dark around it, while it stayed light. I considered that the light from the marquees never went down, never went out.

I was philosophical like that. I drank. I didn't think about Cambridge anymore. I didn't think about my stories anymore. I didn't even think about the Thayer case. There'd be time enough for that tomorrow. I thought about Olivia . . . about my ex-wife Constance and my late kid Olivia. I thought about the people I'd known—the cops, and the junkies, and the husbands on the run—who had died alone in one-bedroom apartments too many flights off the street, where the shadows

gather and the dust collects and the paint chips on the wall.
I thought about that. I thought about Constance. I thought
about Olivia. I drank.

I was twenty-three years old when I met her. One of the
stables of her parents' horse farm burned down. I was working
up in northern Westchester on a little daily near Mt. Kisco:
a one-room operation. I was a reporter, a photographer, and
an editor sometimes too.

I was the eager type. Eager to work through the night,
eager to see my byline on the front page in the morning.
Eager to seem cool and tough and not too eager.

Just six months before, I'd come into town on a freight
out of Maine. My father was a forest ranger up there. He'd
died fighting a fire. Nothing heroic, just lost it to the smoke.
I think he must have figured it was the easier way—easier,
I mean, than hanging around to watch the cancer kill my
mother. He left me to do that. And I left my brother and
sister to bury her. Never saw them again.

I got off the freight when it stopped heading south. It
was New York City or bust for me. I unrolled my clean set
of clothes and walked till I came to a little city. I got a job
at the launderette next door to the paper. The paper gave me
stringer work when they saw I could write. Then they hired
me a month later.

I didn't know what had hit me. The job grabbed me from
the start. It was a job I could work from the minute I got up
in the morning till the minute I went to bed the morning after.
It was good work, smart work, work you had to think about.
I thought about it. I didn't think about where I'd come from.
I didn't think about where I'd go. I thought about getting the
story. I learned to get the story.

So the story that cold, clear January night was the burning
stables, the screaming horses, the wealthy family out maybe
millions in Saratoga speed. I was alone in the office battering
out a town board meeting when I heard the call on the police
scanner. I grabbed the camera and ran out back to my car.
A hook-and-ladder went screaming by as I pulled out into
the street. I attached myself to its rear fender and followed
it to the scene.

What a scene it was too. It was a crystal, starry winter's night. No moon at all. A glittering sky hung over the county's tree-lined horizon. To the south I could see it, that sky. Down from the hill where the Brett farm stood, it spread out peaceful as prayer song, like an old world country at the end of a fairy-tale road. In the north, though, it had been obliterated. In the north the red flames vaulting from the stable's roof erased it. The red flasher lights from the dozen engines beat it into nothingness. I jumped out of my car, dragging the camera behind me. I ran, wild-eyed, into the center of chaos.

Now, there is something about a camera. Any newsman will tell you. It does something to you to look at a story through a lens. I have seen men not otherwise brave stand up in the middle of a police crossfire or a riot or a hostage showdown just to get a good picture for the front page. I once saw a woman who could not bear the sight of blood walk through the carnage of a train wreck snapping off shots, unmoved. The camera puts the world at arm's length. Makes it distant, unreal. The lens is a cold eye to cast on death for those who haven't got one of their own, and the bravest cameramen I've ever met have all been cowards under the skin.

So I got out of my car and I slapped the camera to my face and I charged into the burning stables.

Everything that happened next happened in snapshots. Shots of the mad white eyes of horses straining through the smoke. Shots of the animals rearing behind a wall of flames. I caught the face of a stable hand, stained with soot, streaked with tears, as he hauled on a rope in a desperate battle to pull a frantic stallion out into the open air. I caught a filly sleek with grace and beauty lifting up screaming out of the blaze as the roof came tumbling down around her. All of it happened, it seemed to me, in still, short bursts of motion. In silence. In pictures inside the camera.

And then, all at once, the roar of the flames broke on top of me like a wave. The smoke overwhelmed me. The stable wheeled and faded and rushed toward me. I thought I saw my father's face. I thought I heard my mother's voice. And, in fact, someone was screaming at me, clawing weakly at my shoulder, trying to turn me around. Dazed, I pivoted, and I saw her.

She was trying to pull me toward the door. She was screaming, "What are you doing? What are you doing here? What are you doing?"

I heard myself laughing. It was a crazy, high-pitched laugh. "I'm taking pictures, man!" I shouted madly. "I'm taking goddamned pictures!"

She got hold of my jacket and pulled. I staggered after her out the door. I fell to the ground, my lungs grabbing at the cool air. My eyes cleared and I saw the sheet of smoke that lay between me and the stars. And I saw her above me too. I saw her swipe the tears from her face with a brusque, angry motion of her arm. I heard her sobbing. The stable hand rushed by her toward the burning structure. She grabbed his arm. She screamed at him:

"William!"

He turned to her and I saw his eyes rolling white in his blackened face. "They're all dying, Miss Brett!" He was gibbering. Spit flew from his mouth, tears sparkled flame red on his cheeks. "They're all dying!"

He tried to pull away from her. She wouldn't let him go.

"Don't die!" she shouted. "Don't die! You can't! . . . It's over! Over . . ."

He tried again to shake her loose. She flung her arms around his neck and wept on his shoulder. It saved his life. He held her, rocking her back and forth. He raised his face to heaven, weeping too.

I lay on the ground beneath the smoke, clutching my camera, watching. I had never seen anything like her in my life.

She herself had the long strong lines of a creature bred for speed. She was tall and slender and sleek, and when I saw her next I saw how her figure flowed inside her jeans and her tan sweater. Her features were small and exquisite and perfectly related, like those of a porcelain figurine that someone has worked on for years. She had long blond hair that fell straight to her shoulders. She had arching eyebrows over dark green eyes. She was eighteen.

She came into the office on a Saturday afternoon two weeks later. Only me and the sports guy were there. He was pounding out the high school scores, I was doing a piece about a back-country road that had frozen over. I felt the cold air from the door. I looked up over my typewriter, and she was there. She stood with her hips slanted. She looked down at me smiling. She was smoking a cigarette. She must have planned it: No one looks that good by accident.

I stood up. She turned around and went back out. I followed her. She walked across the parking lot. It was nice to watch. The winter sun was low in the sky, a pale disk. I saw its reflection on the polished hood of her car. The car was red. It was low and racy. Something Italian.

She got in behind the wheel. I got in on the passenger's side. I watched her profile as she shot the machine out into the street.

She went easily through town, she didn't push it. But when the buildings faded away beside us, when the road began to twist into the hills and the woods, her foot sank down on the pedal. The speedometer needle climbed steadily. The trees at the windows became a blur. But it was all so silent. The engine hummed. The tires never screeched on the hairpin turns. It was all so elegant and so dangerous. I was twenty-three. I thought it was the greatest thing ever.

I didn't say anything. That was part of it, I guess: whether I would say anything or not. I didn't. I lit a cigarette. She turned to me and smiled.

She took me over a dirt road, deep into the land her father owned. He owned all the land around the farm. Rolling hills for horses. We came to the brink of a sort of tor, fringed with trees. The trees were bare. We looked through their branches, down at the shambles of the stable that had burned. She turned off the engine.

I looked down at the charred black stain of the wreckage on the pale brown hill below. I smoked. I finished my cigarette. I put it out in the ashtray open on the dash.

Constance turned to me. She brushed her hair out of her face. She smiled. I felt like I was back in the burning stable again: my chest was heavy; I couldn't breathe.

She laughed a little. She shook her head. "Taking god-damned pictures," she said.

And then I couldn't stop kissing her.

* * *

It was like that for a year, maybe a year and a half.
Every day, all day, she would be with me in sudden flash-
backs. Frozen, fragmentary memories of the night before that
would take me over for seconds at a time, that would leave
me, when they faded, staring at a pale, distant reality that
was not as real as she was. I would be interviewing the
superintendant of highways about the shortfall of the sand
budget when, suddenly, in my mind, he would fade away
from me and I would be tasting the surface of her belly. I
would be watching the town supervisor cut the ribbon on a
waste treatment plant and then, all at once, I'd be somewhere
else. I would feel her fingernails raking my back; I'd feel
them reaching up into my hair. Or I would be waking up
some police dispatcher for the morning cop calls and I would
be inside her, I would feel her breath in my mouth as she
cried out, I would hear her. "Anything happen overnight?"
I'd ask the cop, and laugh.

Still, still and all, we never would have gotten married
if her old man had liked me. He was a crusty, gray-haired
buzzard who wore smoking jackets a lot. He couldn't tolerate
"the differences in our upbringing." I was worse than lower
class, I guess. I was middle class. And he gave her hell about
it. Anyway, we got married in what Constance later said was
"a fit of pique," which I guess about describes it. I remember
her yanking her short-cut riding jacket off a chair and saying,
"I've really just about had it with that bastard." Her father,
she meant. "Let's just get married. That should shut him up."

I was the one who should have known better. I wasn't
angry. I didn't give a damn what her father thought of me. I
didn't give a damn about anything except the taste and the
feel and the cries of her. So if instead of "Let's get married,"
she'd said, "Let's murder the old man," her father wouldn't
have made it through the night. As it was, a justice of the
peace had us hitched before the week was over.

Two months later she was pregnant. I don't know if it
was an accident. I don't know if it ever is, if anything ever
is. All I know is it was fine with me. I'd just gotten a job in
White Plains with the top-dog paper there. The word was out

on me. It was a good word and I knew it. So things were fine and I was thrilled when she told me.

I laughed and said, "Oh man, that's great, that's great."

She reared up to her full height. Her mouth was slack at the corners. The pouches under her eyes were gray. She looked down her well-bred nose at me. "You don't really think I'm going to keep it, do you?" she said.

Well, we had it out. We took it around the block and back again. It was the only fight we ever had, and it was a battle royal. I won it finally. She was slumped on the floor in tears. I was hunched forward in the easy chair with my face in my hands. "All right. All right," she said, and I had won. I've often thought about that, about how I won. I would not have won if it had happened even five years later. Already by then I would have known better than to win.

But I won, and we had Olivia, and she lived for fifteen years and then she died. She was an assistant counselor at a summer camp when it happened. She got up before dawn one morning in the barracks she supervised. She had this stuffed giraffe one of the younger girls coveted. She left it on the bunk beside the child and walked off into the night. They found her late in the morning. She was hanging from the branch of a tree. She'd used the rope from a tent to do it. So I guess that's what I won her.

For myself, I won the best two years of my life. Those first two years of Olivia. There's been nothing like them since. Even the crying in the middle of the night made me glad. When she took her first step, I handed out cigars. I made everyone look at the pictures of her stumbling along. They slapped my back and cast sidelong glances at each other and heavenward. I didn't notice. When I did notice, I didn't care. I loved that kid. I loved that little kid. I didn't notice anything but her.

I didn't, for instance, notice Constance. I tried to, but she wouldn't let me, and after a while I decided that was just as well. She'd hired a maid to take care of the kid when I was at work. When I was at home, she let me do it. I chose not to see her sullen, gray sinking into bitterness. I chose not to hear her sarcasms and her self-abrasions. I chose not to smell the booze, or think about the absent afternoons when

I could not find her. I played with Olivia. I changed her. I tickled her. I fed her. I laughed like a loon when she said my name. And then one day my wife left me, and took the kid with her. Not as fast as that, but just about.

There wasn't much of a court fight. In those days the mother just pretty much got the kid. I myself thought that was the way it ought to be. It wasn't until years later that I reconsidered, and by then it was too late. Constance had gone to Europe by then, to the south of France. It was against our settlement, but I couldn't stop her. She never denied me visitation rights. I just couldn't afford to take advantage of them very often. I wrote as much as I could. When Olivia was old enough to answer, she always did. I think about that a lot too. She always answered me. By then her mother hated me almost insanely. She hated me for giving her Olivia. And sometimes, I think, she hated Olivia too. But Olivia kept writing me, and her letters began "Dear Daddy," and they ended with love, and I think about that as often as I can bear.

I remember, in fact, when Constance called me, that's what I did: I went to the letters. I listened to Constance tell me in her dull, hollow, shocked voice. I shook my head quietly to myself as she spoke. I remember I was half smiling, the way I've seen guys do just after they've been sucker punched, and just before they drop to the ground unconscious. I remember then I went to the closet, to the shoe box in the closet where I kept the letters. They were tied in a bundle. I took the bundle out. I dragged a bottle to the desk and poured myself a long drink. A night-long drink. I drank and I untied the bundle. I read the letters over, one by one.

I guess I was looking for clues. I guess I was asking myself: Should I have known? Could I have? She never wrote to me in anguish or despair—not that I could tell anyway. She never complained, she never cried out. I read those letters over and over. There was only this, at the very end. Only one letter, in which the tone of quiet, thoughtful consideration was unlike her. In which—if I had known her better—I might have recognized an argument against her own dark pressures, a last attempt to unravel the night inside her.

I sat at the table and I drank and I read that last letter.

I have been thinking about things a lot lately, Daddy. About life, I guess. I've been thinking about how to live. It seems to me that people think of life as a fair deal, even though they know it's not deep down. They think if they handle things just so, just right, everything will be fine. I used to think that, I know, when I was little. I used to think if I could just be good, if I could just be good enough, you and Mommy would get back together and everything would be all right again. It took a long time before I realized that wasn't so. Part of growing up, I guess. But the thing is, I've just been thinking that life isn't really like that at all. It isn't fair or unfair or nice or not nice. It just is: and that's the whole beauty of it. And, if you want to live, to live well, to live life the way life can be lived, then I think you've got to love life for what it really is, just for the fact that it is, not for what it's supposed to be. You have to love life with all the dying and the pain of it, with all the good-byes and the hurting inside. You have to love mourning the way you love joy, because there can't be one without the other. You have to love death the way you love life, because in the end, they're really all one thing. Because even if it isn't fair or unfair, it's sweet, I think. I think maybe it's sweet as wine.

I've been thinking about that a lot. I've really been pushing myself on it. I've really just been telling myself: love life as it is, Olivia. You have to love life as it is.

I sat and I read that letter and drank. I sat where I was sitting now. I drank as I was drinking now: to kill the pain. Now, though, the pain was different. Five years had passed and made it different. I do not think it had grown any more bearable. I simply had grown better at bearing it. That's not quite the same thing.

So now, after a while, I stopped thinking of my little girl. I sat with my feet on the desk and the glass balanced on my belt buckle. I stared out the window at the movie marquee. Still bright, still bright. Around it full night had fallen.

The scotch filled me up. It made me warm inside. Warm and cold at the same time, sort of like wintergreen on the tongue. The warmth was all the tight places relaxing. The cold was all the hurt places cauterized. I could keep it that way for another hour, I figured, and that was fine with me.

I sat and I drank and I stared and soon I saw a face. I saw it float and fade on the darkened air before me. A girl's face. A pretty face. Enough, I thought to myself. Enough. But it wasn't her. It wasn't Olivia. It was Michelle.

Michelle had also been found hanging in the woods. But her mother said it was murder. Now, with a little help from Cambridge, the *Star* had proclaimed pretty much the same thing. And it occurred to me, as I sat growing wise with each passing sip of whiskey . . . it occurred to me that maybe I had known it would happen that way. I couldn't find any rational reason to investigate this case. So maybe I let Cambridge muck it up. Maybe I wanted it that way so I could get all riled and force him to let me investigate. Maybe, oh yeah, maybe I had it figured somewhere deep down from the minute I spoke to Mrs. Thayer: if Cambridge played her accusations up, as he was almost sure to, then I could investigate. I could investigate—and I could find out that it was murder.

Because Lansing was right: if it was murder, I could find the killer.

And if I found him, I could make him pay.

I thought about that. I thought about Michelle. I stared out the window. I drank.

18

My welcome to Grant County wasn't as warm the second time. I holed up in the same hotel. Drove the same road to the same high school. I went to the same office to meet with the same principal. But the look on his face was not the same.

The firm, sincere, blue eyes of David Brandt looked sternly out of his pale handsome face. I would have quailed if I was the quailing type.

"Listen—" I said. I held up my hand.

"If you're not off this school's grounds in five minutes, I'm calling the police."

I thought about Tammany Bird. I have to admit, I quailed a little then.

"Listen—" I said.

"This school—this entire community—trusted you. We trusted you with our stories. We trusted you with our grief. The way you handled that trust, the way you abused it . . . I can't begin to tell you the potential for damage there."

"Listen—" I said.

"But even if there were not that potential, simple moral grounds, I would think, would have precluded your handling these stories as you did."

This, I could tell, was a man who had never worked with an editor.

There was no explaining either. He slammed his office door in my face. The secretaries eyed me crossly with tight lips. I thought one of them would shake a finger at me. I wondered where you showed up for detention around here.

I went outside. It was early in the morning. The kids were just filing over the front yard and into school. The sun was dodging the big clouds of November that surged over it and passed away again in the chilly wind. The wind also made the dying leaves fall and the fallen leaves whirl above the ground.

I stood for a moment and watched the traffic passing on the main road. I could sense the glares I was getting from the kids passing on every side of me. I had that nervous, excited feeling I get when I know I am in hostile territory.

And then the traffic disappeared from in front of me. In front of me there was nothing but the color blue. I stepped back. The blue was the blue of a school jacket. There was an orange G sewn on its breast. A very large young man was inside the jacket. Two other very large young men were in similar jackets behind him.

The large young man who had stepped in front of me was a trim broad-shouldered giant with a clean-cut handsome face, trim black hair, and a few pimples on his chin.

He said, "You're that reporter."

I nodded.

"I think what you wrote about Michelle Thayer stinks," he said. "I'd like to bash your fucking head in."

"The story was rewritten by my editor, Robert Cambridge," I said. I gave him Cambridge's home address.

"If you weren't such an old fuck, I *would* bash your head in."

"C-A-M-B-R-I-D-G-E," I said.

"Go ahead," said one of the large young men behind the large young man. "Go ahead, bash his fucking head in."

I didn't like the sound of that. It was beginning to become a leitmotif. What's more, the students who had been moving toward the door had now stopped to watch. I could see them out of the corner of my eye. They were inching toward us. The expression on each of their faces was the same: an expression of grim approval. Justice, they figured, was about to be done.

As the kids began to gather, the large young man who had stepped in front of me began to gather courage. He hadn't really meant to bash my head in when he started. But now —with all those grimly approving faces around—the idea was sounding better and better to him all the time.

"Listen—" I said.

But I wasn't having much luck with that argument today. The large young man shot his right arm out. He hit me in the left shoulder with the heel of his palm. I let out a breath and took a step backward. The students all around us stirred with excitement and approval.

"Shut up," the large young man told me.

This seemed to me to be getting out of hand. I tried a new argument.

"Lookit—"

"I said shut up."

The large young man shot his arm out at my shoulder again. I knew he was going to do this: He did not strike me as endlessly creative. So when he shot his arm out at my collar again, I dropped back on my heel and pivoted down and away. His hand flew over my collar. He was off balance. He came forward a step. I straightened and put my hand on his collar gently. I put my hand on his collar, and my thumb on his throat. I did not press my thumb into his throat. I hardly touched it at all. I didn't have to. I could see in the sudden, fearful widening of his eyes that he got the message.

He straightened up. I kept my hand on his collar. I took my thumb off his throat. I grinned.

"My friend," I said between my teeth. He nodded, his eyes still wide. I went on, softly, so those around us would not hear. "My friend, I have lived quite a while," I said, "and several people have tried to kill me. Some of them killed people for a living. But I am still here. Consider this."

He did. I watched him consider it while we stood there together, he staring past me with his wide eyes, me with my hand on his collar, fatherly. He considered this, and I think the idea of bashing my face in began to lose its appeal.

His eyes refocused on me. "Why don't . . . why don't you just . . . why don't you just, I mean, get out of here," he said. "Okay?"

I took back my hand. I shrugged. "Sure," I said.

He motioned with his head at the two large young men behind him. The three of them strode past me toward the school. One of them bumped into me as he passed.

I sighed. All around me I sensed an answering sigh. The

students were breaking it up, moving away. They did not know whether to be sorry or relieved that it had come to nothing. I, for one, was relieved.

I'd parked the Artful Dodge on the street. I walked down the high school path toward it. I had reached the sidewalk before I felt someone grab my arm at the elbow. I was annoyed.

"Aw, come on, man," I said, turning. "Get smart."

But it was not the large young man. It was another young man: a thin, almost anemic creature, maybe sixteen, with wide, riveting brown eyes in a long, white face. He was dressed in a black shirt and black jeans. His black hair was cut to the nub. He kept his hand on my elbow. He kept his eyes on my eyes.

The minute I saw him something went through me, something chill and electric. It snaked quickly up my spine. It blossomed in my brow and vanished. It was something very much like fear.

"At the corner of Farm-to-Market and Bullethole Road . . ." he said.

His voice was nearly a whisper. It had no substance at all. I did not like the sound of his voice.

"Walk northeast into the woods, up the hill. There's a root cellar there. At five o'clock."

I stared at him. I didn't answer. He studied me with wild eyes.

"All right?" he said. "All right?"

"Secret meetings are my life," I said.

"Just be there, all right?"

"All right."

"Because she was, you know." He said it urgently. His eyes would not let me go. "She was."

"Was what?" I said.

"Murdered."

He finally released me.

"Oh," I said.

And he turned and walked away.

19

At four-thirty I was there. The corner of Farm-to-Market and Bullethole Road was a desolate spot. It was the crossing of two lonesome roads: two roads that dipped and lifted through hills of trees and vanished into the horizons on every side. I parked the car, got out and stood beside it. I peered into the woods. Northeast, he'd said.

The sun had just dropped below the horizon. The light was fading on the naked trees. During the brief time I had been in the city, autumn had crossed the line. The trees that had been full of color were bare or in the rags of that color now. Their branches swayed in the wind of the gloaming. The woods seemed very dark and very bleak.

I started walking. There wasn't much of a path. The woods rose up around me in a steep hill. I was out of breath quickly. I kept lifting my eyes from the humus beneath my shoes to the deepening forest dark around me. I couldn't see the root cellar. I couldn't see much of anything. The moon had not yet risen into the intermittent clouds.

I climbed some more. The dead leaves crunched beneath my feet. The sound of my breath overwhelmed them. I cursed the day I started smoking. The hill's peak loomed above me: hulking trees silhouetted on the purple sky.

Then I was among those trees. I pushed the branches from my face. I crested the hill. There was the moon, low on the slope of the next hill over. A full moon. I saw the root cellar in its silver light. I saw the young man.

His face was chalk white in the new moonlight. His black clothes blended into the forest dark. I remembered the sight of Death by the stone wall outside of the Thayer house. And I felt that shiver once again.

The root cellar was just an old domed structure of stone, of one stone piled on another. He stood beside it, leaning against it with his elbow, like a man showing off his new house in a snapshot. I went down the hill toward him.

He didn't move as I approached. He stood there. He stared. It was the same when I was face to face with him. It kind of unnerved me. I took a cigarette from my pocket and lit it. I hid behind the match flame. I shook out the match and blew smoke into the air. I hid behind the smoke.

"All right," I said. "You're sylvan and mysterious. I'm John Wells."

Weird as he was, he smiled. He inclined his head. He spoke again in that eerie whisper. "Chris Thomas," was all he said.

"Okay, Chris. Let's have it."

I saw his eyes glitter. He found the whole thing exciting. "She used to come here . . . to the cellar," he said.

"Michelle Thayer."

"Yes. She used to come here to be with me."

I glanced from him to the little domed hut. "That's where she went after school, you mean."

He paused. He gave a single, abrupt nod. "Yes."

"She was—"

"Well, sometimes."

"Okay, she came here sometimes. She was your girl-friend."

He laughed. I couldn't see his face much anymore, just the white sheen of it in the moon. It seemed a floating haze above his black clothes. He laughed and said: "No. Not really. I mean . . . well . . . I loved her. But . . . not really." He turned away from me. Even in the dark it was a bashful gesture. He stepped around the corner of the cellar, out of my sight. I followed him. He was gone. There was a low arched doorway into the cellar. I ducked under the lintel stone and went in.

Now I could not see him. Now, in fact, I couldn't see anything. Nothing but the moon through the arch of the doorway and the standing, wavering trees outside. Nothing but the tip of my cigarette as it glowed on a breath before me.

"Okay," I said. "You're invisible now. Tell me."

"We didn't come here to . . . We came here to talk."

"You weren't lovers?"

I sensed his shudder in the dark. "I loved her, but she . . ."

I waited. "Loved someone else?"

"Yes."

"Who?"

"Death."

I followed the sound of his voice and grabbed him. He cried out. I took hold of his lapel and twisted him around into the moonlit doorway.

"Enough of this," I said. "Let me see your face. Was it you? Out in the caves? Death in the woods. All that? Was it you?"

For a moment there was nothing but his heavy breathing. I released my hold on him. He sagged against the doorway. I tossed my cigarette to the ground and crushed it under my feet. He was the second kid I'd roughed up today. I was a very proud man.

I raised my face to him. "Was it you?" I said more gently.

"No. It was Death. She loved Death. That's why she went to that place. That's why she worked at that place all the time."

"What place?"

"The hotline. Where the people called. She wanted to hear them talk about it."

"A phone hotline."

"Yes."

"For what? For the suicidal?"

"Yes."

"There is none in this area. I checked."

"It was over the line."

"The line?" I hadn't thought of that. "In Connecticut?"

He nodded. "Brentford. She took a bus there. Once a week. That's where she went. She never told anyone."

"She told you."

He straightened. "She told me everything," he said proudly.

I sighed. I reached out and patted his shoulder with my hand. "I'm sorry," I said.

He spoke unsurely. "Something's . . . wrong with you, isn't it? You're mad—pissed. . . ."

"Yeah. That's right."

"Because she was murdered."

"Maybe. If she was. Maybe that's part of it."

He hesitated. He considered, I think, whether to speak. Then he said: "The rest of them don't understand. You understand, don't you? About Death, about loving Death?"

I didn't answer. "It's almost dinnertime," I said. "Let me drive you home."

I saw him tremble in the darkness, like a deer. He shook his head. Then he turned around, and before I could reach for him again, he was loping away into the night.

20

I drove back to town. I stopped off in a convenience store and dialed Connecticut information. I got the number for the hotline and called. The line was busy. I had a cup of coffee and tried again. The line was still busy. I smoked a cigarette out in the parking lot. I tried again. Busy. I called information to see if the hotline's address was listed. It was. It was in the Church of St. Andrew, on Briar Road. I climbed back into the Artful Dodge.

The road to Connecticut wound through the woods—like most of the roads around here, it seemed. The night mist was now curling out of the forests, curling up to the edges of the pavement, lying across the pavement in a thin sheet. It glowed in my headlights.

It seemed I drove for a long time. Anything can be a long time on those roads. They twist and turn, but they never change. The trees and the darkness haunt them. You can go for miles without seeing a light—even a stoplight—even a house set back in the woods. If you think you're lost, if you think you might run out of gas, if your car breaks down, you feel like you're a hundred miles away from anywhere. But if you stand very still in the night and listen, you will hear the whisper of other cars on other roads nearby, twisting and turning through the woods that never change.

I saw a small sign welcoming me across the border. That was the only difference between one state and another.

Brentford is a fairly large little city. Maybe fifty thousand souls. I never got to the center of it, though. I was in the outskirts, among large houses on even larger tracts of land, when I found the Brentford R.C. Church of St. Andrew.

It was an old, crumbling structure set on top of a rocky hill. It looked deserted. Its boards, once white, were brown. They sagged. Its steeple was chipped, so you could see the rafters. There were no lights inside, just the moon's strange glow on the rose window above the front door. The church squatted above me as I came up its winding drive.

There were no other cars parked at the top. I was sure I was in the wrong place. After I had stepped into the chill night, after the car door had thudded shut behind me, the silence seemed to creep out of the dark to surround the place like the Indians in an old cowboy film. I walked over a path of pebbled gravel to the decrepit church. I went up the stairs and stood before two large, brass-studded wooden doors. I touched the wood. The door swung in, creaking loudly. I nearly laughed at the horror-movie sound effect. Nearly. I stepped inside. The door creaked and swung back in.

The air was filled with a musty smell of candles and decay. I was in the dark. Almost the dark. On the walls at either side of me, peaked, stained-glass windows glowed with the moon. I could make out the ghostly blue shadow of St. Andrew, his head flung back, his mouth jacked wide in agony, his hands and feet nailed to his X-shaped cross. I could make out the somber kings—red and white and yellow—bringing gifts to Bethlehem. I could make out the raging scarlet angel blowing the last trump. I thought I saw the eyes of the devil burning silver with the moon.

I called out: "Hello."

No one answered. I shuffled forward a little. A little more. I listened. I thought I heard faint voices in the empty room. I never have liked churches. They give me the willies.

My eyes were adjusting now to the dark. I could make out the shapes of the pews. There weren't many. Most of the places where they had been seemed stripped bare. In another moment I saw the altar. I saw the crucified Christ gleaming faintly on the wall above it. Some sort of complex wooden altarpiece seemed to be hanging atilt next to it. It seemed to have fallen into disrepair.

I scanned the room slowly. I saw a movement to the left of the altar. Curtains, I thought, stirring in the night air.

Behind them I caught a glimpse of an even deeper darkness. I shuffled forward down the aisle.

The voices in the emptiness around me grew louder. Low, murmuring voices. I reached the curtain and pulled it back. I walked into the darkness behind.

There was a hallway. I couldn't see much of it. I came forward with my hand against a wall. My fingers touched a metal door. I stood and listened. The voices were coming from behind it.

I opened the door. Black, it was utterly black in there. Then I made out stairs, rickety stairs leading downward. I hate churches. I always have.

I went down the stairs. The murmuring voices got louder. My feet touched down on stone. I was in the cellar of the place. I was disoriented by the completeness of the dark.

I called out: "Hello!"

The light flashed out at me. It hit me like the edge of a sword. I was blinded. I put my hand up before my eyes.

"Yes?"

It was a woman's voice. I saw her silhouette in the doorway that had just opened in front of me. For a long moment the blinding light kept me from seeing anything else. Squinting, my hand still raised as a shield, I came forward.

"Yuh—yes . . ." She stammered this time, uncertain, and something about her voice made me pause. It was familiar to me. It seemed to have spoken out of the memories of the night before. Now, standing there, surprised and still, I heard her slight intake of breath: a startled sound, a sound of recognition.

I came forward. I saw the room behind her. A desk. Figures in there, hunched over the phones. Then she stepped back from me, unsteadily. She nearly staggered back and, as she did, the light came down across her face.

I stopped in my tracks. I lowered my hand.

"I know you," I said.

She answered quietly, but her face was pale: "Yes, John."

"Chandler Burke," I said.

And she answered: "Yes."

21

She was wearing a simple, tan skirt and a prim, high-collared blouse of white lace. She wasn't a beautiful woman. She never had been. Her face was too pale, and her pale eyes were saggy and sad. Her hair was a lackluster brown. It framed her cheeks shapelessly. There was now, too, a spinsterly tightness to her thin, white lips, a nervous shifting of her eyes, quick, stealthy gestures of her slender hands that I'd never seen before. Her figure, though, remained nearly as it was: full and soft. It seemed it would be warm to the touch.

I'd known her only briefly, and that almost eighteen years ago.

She'd worked in White Plains then. She was a social worker, a counselor at a clinic for substance abusers. I'd worked with her when I did a story on heroin addiction. She'd given me a guided tour of the city's shooting galleries and hit joints. I remember her soft, nervous, girlish voice describing the horrors there.

I saw her maybe nine, ten times in the course of a few months. That's all. But she had those sad, understanding eyes and a sympathetic little tilt to her head when she was listening . . . and she listened well. My marriage was falling apart, and I'd finally caught on. Constance was going to take my kid away from me. I knew it. I was broken-hearted and desperate, and I didn't know where to turn.

One day Chandler was guiding me through a city hospital ward. Past heavy doors, shut tight. Past screened windows. Screaming, cold-turkey faces pressed to the glass. Hands like claws scrabbling. Muffled voices begging for a fix, mad for it. On she went, in that liquid murmur. And I found myself studying her white lips, the shape of them. The shape of her neck when her hair moved away from it. She glanced at me, caught me at it. She held my sorry gaze a moment, then looked away. Went on talking. I felt like an idiot, like an erring husband in a bad movie. One of those fifties jobs where it's all done without skewing the knot in your tie.

We came to the end of the hospital corridor. We pushed out into a stairwell. I followed her down until we reached the door to the main floor.

"Let me buy you a beer," I said. I cleared my throat.

She hesitated a minute. Then she nodded once without saying a word.

So I bought her a beer at a nearby tavern. A little pub, all glittering bottles and gleaming wood. Watered booze in the bottles. Cigarette burns in the wood. We sat at a table by the window and I bought her a beer and I told her everything. Just like the movie. I started out showing her pictures of my little girl. She tilted her head at them, smiled and cooed.

"And that's my wife," I said, pointing to the shot in my wallet.

She stopped smiling. "She's very beautiful."

That was all it took. I told her how I'd met her, fell for her. About having the kid and what it had done to us. I went on a long time. The beer's last foam dissolved at the bottom of our glasses. The barkeep eyed us grumpily. I just kept going on.

"She drifts. She drifts away," I said. "Like someone on a tide. And I reach for her, and she doesn't . . . she just keeps drifting. Staring at me with these angry eyes, never reaching back." I stared at my empty hand, open on the tabletop. "Just drifting."

Chandler didn't offer me any advice. I hadn't asked for any. She listened until I ran out of steam. When I was finally done talking, I sat across the table from her, stared at my palm a few seconds longer. I caught myself. I snorted. "Jesus," I said. " 'My wife doesn't understand me.' I guess you've never heard that before."

I had started to withdraw my hand when she reached out

and took hold of it. I looked up at her. I saw her eyes soften as she studied me.

My fingers folded over her hand. "Let's get out of here," I said. I was hoarse when I said it.

There was a park nearby. Not much. A square of yellow-green grass with streets slashing the corners, traffic slashing the streets. We walked over a concrete path until we were standing under an old sycamore. Its branches sagged, half strangled by the fumes from the cars. We faced each other. She waited. I took her by the waist and brought her to me. I meant to kiss her lightly, but I was surprised by the force of my hunger, and hers. Suddenly she was pressed hard against me and my mouth was over hers and our tongues were together. Her hands were on my shoulders, my neck, my cheeks. Mine caressed her everywhere.

I pulled back from her, breathless. I opened my mouth, but couldn't speak. Her eyes went over me, searching me out. I looked away.

She let me go.

"Damn," I said. "Damn."

"It's all right," she whispered.

"No. No, it's not."

She didn't answer.

"Chandler. I have to . . ."

She nodded.

"I have to see it to the end. However it goes, I've got to."

"I know that."

"I didn't mean—"

"I know."

I ran my fingers up through my hair. "I'll walk you back to your office."

"No. Thank you. I can manage." Now, when she looked at me, I saw what she felt. How much she felt. Just then she couldn't hide it. She walked away instead.

That was the last time I saw her.

It was odd, I guess, as these things go, odd that I had just been thinking of those days. Or maybe it wasn't so odd.

I think of them often. I even think of her from time to time.
Not many women have looked at me that way. I knew it was
a look that didn't come easily to her, that wouldn't pass away
quickly. But it was a long time ago, anyhow.

Now, in the church cellar, I came toward her, extending
my hand. Her palm was cool and dry.

"Strange world," I said.

And she echoed my thought of a moment before. She
said: "Not so strange really."

She gestured me into the lighted room.

It was a pretty shabby place. Walls of white plaster,
warped with the shape of the stone cellar. There was a bulletin
board hanging to my right papered with flyers of yellow, blue,
pink, and green. As for the rest of the place, it was covered
over with newspaper clippings. My gaze passed briefly over
the headlines: they were stories of suicide, or of rescues from
suicide, or snippets from advice columns dealing with despair, that sort of thing.

There was a cot against the wall to my right. Against the
wall to my left was a desk with a typewriter. It was covered
with papers. The central piece of furniture, though, was the
long table I'd seen from the door. There were three phones
on it and three people sitting in front of the phones, talking
into the phones. Two women, one man, all in their twenties.
Theirs were the voices I'd heard murmuring upstairs. Now I
heard them more distinctly.

"Why do you say that?" one of them asked.

"How long have you felt that way?" said another.

"I'm glad you called. You sound very unhappy," said
the third.

Even down here it sounded like ghostly prayer.

Then Chandler said, "Well, John, what brings you here?"
I opened my mouth to answer. But before I could, she laughed.
It was a quick, nervous laugh, not altogether pleasant. "That's
a silly question," she said. "A story brings you here. What
else?"

I nodded. "Michelle Thayer."

I saw her eyebrows raise a little. "You have a knack for
the sad ones, don't you?"

"Good news is no news," I said. "How have you been, Chandler?"

"Very well, thanks. You?" She could not hold my gaze. Her eyes flitted this way and that. Finally, she glanced off at the typewriter desk.

"I get by," I said.

"Your daughter?"

I paused. "She died."

She looked up quickly. "Oh no, John." She reached out to touch my arm, but she did not. She grew self-conscious suddenly. Her hand fell away.

"It was a long time ago," I said. "She killed herself."

"I'm so sorry."

"Me too. But . . . I wanted to talk to you about Michelle. I understand she used to work here."

"Yes, she was one of my first volunteers when we started up last year."

"This is a hotline? A suicide hotline?"

"Well . . . just a place for people to call when they get depressed or . . . I thought . . . When I was transferred up to northern Westchester—oh, it's about five or six years ago now —I began to see the need for something like it in the area. I wanted to get out of the system and work on my own, anyway, so . . ." That was the way she spoke: diffidently. Her sentences kept trailing off. Her eyes kept slipping away from me. She said: "It took me this long to get funding. . . . The director . . . me . . . I'm the only paid position here." She laughed a little. "And I just get enough to pay my rent . . . feed my cat. . . ." I pictured her alone in her apartment with her cat. She flushed. She knew what I was thinking. "Anyway . . ." she said.

"All the recent suicides should help you get funding anyway."

She nodded, gulping dryly. "Uh, well, the need is more obvious now. As you can see . . ." She gestured toward the volunteers at the table. "The lines are always busy." Her hand wavered in the air. She took hold of it with her other, folded the two on her skirt as if to keep them in place. In her prim, high-collared blouse, she looked just then the very picture of the nervous spinster-woman.

That moment—that last moment of connection between us so long ago—hung between us now like an unfinished sentence. That's what was shaking her up, I knew. And the long pause was making it worse.

"So, uh, what's your theory about all this?" I said, just to say something. "What makes these kids do it . . . all together like that?"

She was grateful. She knew where she was now: Back before that old moment, back to playing the expert to my reporter. Back on safe ground.

She lifted her shoulders a little, a gesture of relief. "They're prone to climates . . . fads, you know. And right now, up here at least, there's a climate of destruction. But it's strictly personal too. I mean, we hear them. . . . They call up here, the kids, and they tell us . . . Well, when they first call, it's always something simple, even silly. Their parents won't let them stay out at night, they have too much homework, or . . . But sooner or later, they tell us about their difficulties with . . . with sex or the, the terrible pressures they're under . . . or the fact that their parents' marriage is—" This time her voice didn't trail off, it stopped abruptly. "You see, each person's problem is individual . . . what's general to them is the attraction toward self-annihilation. A sort of . . . plague of spiritual emptiness, I think. . . ." She huffed like a proper New England schoolmarm. "But I don't suppose that will sell many papers, will it?"

"Beats me. I get paid no matter how many papers they sell."

"Well, there are more . . . substantial reasons, if you like. Sociological reasons . . . I suppose that's what you'd call them."

"Okay."

"Do you want to take notes?"

I shook my head. "It stunts the imagination."

She didn't even smile. "The people who move up here . . . well, they move, you know, to get away, mostly . . . from cities. They move for their children's sakes. Ironically." She drew a deep breath. It only trembled slightly coming out. "But, of course, if you want to live in the . . . in the country, you have to keep it . . . the country. So they zone their houses for large plots of land, acreage that . . . poorer people can't afford. And they—they veto mass transportation plans that might attract those people. Did you try to take a bus here?"

"No, I have a car."

"Most people do. The buses are few and far between. So teenagers too young to drive are left stranded. They have virtually nothing to do but . . . hang out or . . . rely on older friends. And older teens who court the attention of younger ones aren't always the best sort of friends to have. And the girls learn what they . . . what the older boys want from them. And the boys learn about drinking and taking drugs." She stopped, eyed me harshly. "So. Anyway. Have you really no better sources these days than aging social workers?"

A small, embarrassed silence followed. It was filled by the soft murmuring of the three people on the phones.

"Michelle Thayer didn't have an older boyfriend," I said. "Didn't take drugs." And then I asked: "Do you mind if I smoke?"

"Yes. I do, actually. I'm sorry. There's no ventilation down here."

I had the cigarette in my hand. I had been tapping it against the face of my watch. I nodded ruefully and stuck it back into my coat pocket.

"No," said Chandler, "she didn't. But then, in other ways, she was a fairly typical case. She had an unhappy home life. Her mother's something of an alcoholic. Her father deserted them, and so on. She had no way to get away from that environment. What made her really typical, though, is the way her mother . . . I can't remember her name . . ."

"Janet."

"Janet. She put Michelle in the position of an adult . . . confided in her, expected her to act responsibly while she acted, well, like a child. It happens all the time, a sort of reversal of roles. The burden on the child is intolerable." She was speaking more fluidly now, easing into her role of expert. Still, she couldn't look at me for long.

"But she worked as a volunteer here."

"Yes. She called here one day, depressed. I handled the phones alone then. I still do, frequently. We talked. After a while I asked her if she would like to come in and see me."

She smiled slightly. "It was a very radical thing to do, especially with her being so young. But . . . I had a sense about her. . . . I put her on the phones, and after just a few trial runs, I could tell she was excellent . . . absolutely excellent with the clients . . . with . . . She was sympathetic, insightful, patient. She was one of the best I've had so far."

"But you say she was suicidal herself . . ."

"Yes . . . Well, working here helped her a good deal. After a while, in fact, she told me that she thought she'd overcome the impulse, although the depressions still bothered her sometimes. I mean, you shouldn't be surprised that . . . I mean, that's why people enter the helping professions in the first place. Because they know what it is to need help. My mother had a drug problem, so I became a drug counselor . . . and so on."

That "and so on" told me a lot. She had become a drug counselor, and now she counseled the suicidal. It told me a lot about her life in the years since I'd seen her last. Again, she knew what I was thinking. Again, she blushed and looked away.

"You sound as if you were very close to Michelle," I said.

She nodded. "I was." That was all she said, and she said it firmly.

"Her mother thinks she was murdered."

"Does she? I would suspect that's denial. It's very common in these cases."

"Yeah. That's what it sounds like to me too." I rubbed my chin. It gave my hand—itching for a cigarette—something to do. "But listen. Why was it all so secret? Her coming here, her working the phones, her friendship with you. Why didn't she tell anyone?"

"Because it was the only thing she had—coming here, me—the only thing she had that was out of her mother's reach. She knew instinctively that her mother would be jealous to discover that not only she, but other people were relying on her. Her mother could be very strict when her interests were threatened. She could easily have forbidden Michelle to come . . . and even made trouble for me. So . . ."

"So," I said.

She tried for a tone of brightness. "So—you're with the *Star* now. I like that paper." I looked at her quickly. Quickly, she looked away. "I've seen your byline," she whispered.

"Yeah," I said softly. "Yeah, I'm with the *Star*. Listen. Listen, Chandler, you wouldn't want—"

"No," she said. "No, I wouldn't."

"Coffee or something."

"No. Thank you, though, for asking. It's very . . . polite of you."

I shrugged. "Well . . ."

"It's good to see you again, John."

"Yeah, sure. Same here."

"I'll . . . I'll watch out for your articles."

I nodded.

"Well . . ." she said.

"Well . . ."

"Be careful on the stairs on your way out."

22

The mist had become a full fog by the time I started my drive back to Grant Valley. As the Artful Dodge descended from the church, the white haze rose up to meet it. It swirled at the windows, pressed against the windshield, danced in the headlights. When I turned onto the road, I could barely see the pavement before me. I could barely see the trees at the edge of the pavement. I kept my speed down to around thirty. I pushed slowly over the twisting highway, leaning forward, straining to see.

So Cambridge would have to print a retraction. There was that anyway. It wasn't much but it was something. I trusted Chandler enough to go with her appraisal of Michelle and believe her when she said it was suicide. Hell, I should have known that anyway. I *did* know it. I had simply let this story get to me, that's all. I had let it get under my skin. I'd let it roil the silt at the bottom of my consciousness. I'd let it open the trapdoor.

I almost groaned as I drove. I didn't want to think about that. I lit a cigarette. It didn't help. I saw Olivia in her wine-dark robe. I saw her ascending the scaffold. I felt the beads of sweat breaking out on my forehead as I thought of her fastening the noose around her neck. I took a long drag of the cigarette. I knew it was coming, any minute now. . . .

But it did not come. Instead, the image was obliterated from my mind by a wild roar that came out of the dark behind me. All at once, the fog back there exploded with light. The light grew brighter. The roar grew louder. And then the fog spat out a pair of headlights. A black car bore down on me over the winding road.

There was no question but that it was after me. I hit the gas pedal without thinking. The Artful Dodge lurched forward. Its tires screamed as it swerved around the bend. The haze was rushing by me on all sides. In my rearview mirror I could see nothing but the two glaring headlamp eyes growing larger and larger as they approached. Through the windshield I could see nothing but my own headlights, diffused on the face of the fog.

I sped up. For a moment the lights behind me fell back a bit. I gripped the wheel and fought against the next curve. Again the tires shrieked and squealed. The night was filled with the angry roar of the car behind me. It shot forward again. Closer and closer. I was outgunned. I didn't have a chance.

The road twisted hard and fast. The Dodge went round. The black car followed. It pulled out beside me and edged forward. I pulled away, but it roared again and caught me at once. Now it nudged my rear fender sharply. The jolt went through the Dodge end to end. I felt it in my teeth as the tires shimmied toward the sloping dirt shoulder. I felt my arms strain as I pulled the old car aright.

The black car crept up further. With a screech and a thud, it hit me again. Around the back door this time. The Dodge slid hard. I couldn't fight it. I felt the tires lose their grip on the road, skid over the dirt. I hit the gas. The Dodge hung on for dear life, kicking rocks up behind it as it muscled its way back onto the road. For another moment it almost seemed like I would pull away from the black car. But once more it let out its angry roar. Once more it came after me.

Now it pulled right up next to me. For one, two, three harrowing seconds, we came swinging around a curve side by side. As the road lashed out straight for a moment, I glanced over at the black beast beside me. The moment I did, its interior light snapped on.

Death was at the wheel.

The grinning skull's head peered at me through the window, through the swirling mist. Even as my mind shouted that it had to be a mask, my foot went out convulsively and hit the brake. The Dodge went into a skid. And Death moved in.

As my rear tires slipped out behind me, he slid his tail over to ram me in front. The Artful Dodge went spinning out of control. Two tires hit the shoulder. The two others lifted into the air. With a sick feeling in my belly, I realized I was going over. Desperately, I wrestled with the wheel. I lost. The roof of the car slammed into the earth. I was hurled toward the passenger side. My fingers were torn from the wheel. My head hit something—I don't know what. Then even the dark went dark around me.

23

I was aware, at first, only of a period of silence. It seemed deep and long as an arctic night. I was thinking, but I did not know what I was thinking. I was seeing, but I did not know what I saw.

There was a thud. It was not far away. It took my mind a second to recognize the sound as that of a car door slamming.

He's coming. Death is coming.

I heard his footsteps on the road.

I blinked. I shook my head. I was looking at the glove compartment. I was lying on my side. I hurt. These facts worked their way into my head as the footsteps moved closer.

I struggled to sit up. My head weighed a ton. My forehead felt damp and viscid. I did not want to know why.

Slowly, now, I remembered that the car had turned over onto the shoulder of the road. It was resting on its right side. The left tires were in the air. The engine had died and one headlight had been smashed. The other was swinging its beam off at a weird angle. That, as far as I could tell, was the only light there was.

I figured if I could reach up to the driver's window, I could lower it and pull myself out. Vaguely, I understood I had to act fast, but for a moment I couldn't think why.

The footsteps, I remembered then. *He's coming.* I struggled to right myself and listened. The footsteps had stopped.

Where is he? Where the hell is he?

"Risk it," I whispered aloud.

I reached up. I had to stretch a little. I worried that the car would topple over, but it seemed firmly planted where it was. My fingers caught the window handle and wrapped around it. I rolled the window down.

Now I had to get my legs underneath me. I had to brace them against the passenger door. *Where are those bloody footsteps? Where are you Death, you wily guy?* I moved my legs gingerly until my feet were resting against the door. I felt a pain in my shin, and I thought: *I'm lucky. Nothing's broken.*

I stretched again, half standing. I reached the window ledge. I pulled. I pulled myself up. It wasn't easy. The skewed car was filled with the sound of my grunting and with the unpleasant little sobbing noises I made. I shifted, quickly, to get my elbows outside. First one, then the other. My head was in the open air. Cool air. It felt good. I shuffled upward, trying to hoist my legs up after me. I dragged myself to the side. My right leg came through; then my left. I'd made it. I was poised on top of the car. I inhaled the piny chill of the November forest.

I slid down the underside of the car. I held on until the last minute, until my feet were only inches off the ground. Then I let myself go. I landed on soft earth, my knees bending. I stumbled a step, but recovered. I stood beneath the upturned car. The mist surrounded me. I could see nothing but the shadows of the trees, a few feet of pavement. The dangling headlight was flickering now and growing dim. It played and danced across the drifting gray.

Death shrieked and a tire iron whistled at me out of the night.

Later on I realized there was an instant when I had seen him. Out of the corner of my eye I had caught the black silhouette of him, and his grinning skull as he stole around the front of the car where the headlight flickered. If it hadn't been that way, if it had been as sudden as it seemed, my brains would have ended up a pink crisscrossing design on the bottom of the Artful Dodge. But I had that instant, and in that instant I went down, squatting. The iron flashed over me. I felt the breeze of it in my hair. It slammed sickeningly into the car. I felt the shock of it in my spine. Death lifted the iron to strike again.

I had planned to spring back up and slug him when he

was off balance. But my knees weren't what they'd been when I was young. My knees, in fact, weren't what they'd been half an hour ago. When I ducked, they gave out on me. I toppled over. I rolled. The tire iron thudded into the mud beside me. Death's head loomed inches from my face. I reached up. My fingertips scraped the latex of his mask. I saw his living eyes through the peepholes. They looked like twin whirlpools of rage.

He pulled away. He raised the tire iron above his head. Once again I rolled. The tire iron struck the edge of the road. I saw sparks fly out from underneath it. I heard Death grunt with the pain of the reverberating blow. I seized the moment and clambered to my feet.

We faced each other in the road. I crouched, my hands up before me. He gripped the tire iron in both hands, waving it at me. He snarled.

"Come on, come on," I hissed at him.

He came. He lunged at me. He jabbed the tire iron at my head. That was a mistake. If he'd gone for my body somewhere, he might have caught me. Instead, I only had to duck slightly to the side. The iron bar went by my ear. His arms were extended beside me. I jabbed upward with the stiffened fingers of my right hand. I hit him in the armpit.

"Aaaaaah!" he said. He stumbled to the side.

"Trick or treat, fuckhead," I gasped. And I charged him.

He was quick. Quicker than I was. He recovered and had the tire iron in front of him. It hit me in the left breast. I coughed and wheeled away as he recovered. I danced back from the point of the thing. It followed after me.

Death advanced. But I could see in the eyes behind the mask that I had hurt him, I had made him think. He was not in such a hurry to come at me now.

For a few breaths we stood challenging each other. I watched his every move as he stood framed against my upturned car.

"Get out," he said. He had a voice like a thumbnail on a blackboard. It was not his normal voice, but it wasn't phony either. It was the sound of the hatred living inside him. It made my throat tighten just to hear it.

"Get out of my county," he said. "Get out."

"Shut up and come for me, you son of a bitch," I said. I was bluffing. My wind was almost gone. My legs felt leaden. I thought I might buy it if he came again.

He didn't, though. He kept the iron in front of him as a defense and he began to back away.

"Get out," he screaked.

I did not follow him. When a few yards separated us, he turned his back on me and ran. He vanished in the mist instantly. I stood still, panting in the dark. I half expected him to come screaming out of the white haze again from another direction. But I heard his car door open now down the road: open and close. I heard his engine cough and roar. I heard the sound of his engine. I heard it click into gear.

I heard it fading away from me. He was gone.

24

"Hm, hm, hm," drawled Tammany Bird. "Hm, hm, hm."

"My sentiments exactly," I said. I lowered myself slowly into the chair across from his desk. My knees were killing me. The cut on my head—cleaned and bandaged now—was throbbing. My chest felt like a flamenco dance floor. The rest of me ached. Even my lungs ached. All of me.

"Hm-dy hm," said Tammany Bird. The giant police chief was stretched out in his reclining chair. His big feet were hoisted up onto his desk. His big hands rested on his big belly. His big chin rested on his big chest. Out of his long face, his transparent eyes studied me.

"Hm-dy hm," I agreed. I avoided his gaze. I stared at the two flags flanking the window behind him: the state flag and the stars and stripes. I wanted a cigarette, but I didn't feel I would survive one. So I just sat there. I waited for him to talk.

"So you have told your story to the officer on the scene," he said.

"I have."

"And you have told your story to B.C.I."

"Yup."

"And now you would like to brighten my evening by sharing it with me."

"Don't you ever go home?" I said.

"Eternal vigilance is the price of something."

"Freedom."

"Right. Here I be."

I spread my hands. "What can I say after I say a man wearing a skull mask tried to kill me?"

He tilted his head. "That would about sum it up."

"Story in a nutshell."

"Admirably concise." He heaved a big sigh. His big chest rose and fell bigly. "What if I asked you to surmise the identity of this man . . . it was a man, you're certain of that."

I considered. "No. Not really. He was wearing a black sweatshirt and black jeans. From what I remember of the shape of him, I'd guess a man. Not to mention his major league way with a tire iron. But not a hundred percent certain, no."

He nodded, scratched his putty nose ham-handedly. "Care to see if you can narrow it down a bit further than that?" he drawled.

"Well . . . It was someone who wants me out of this county."

Bird startled me with a large, rasping laugh. His feet came down off the desk, crashed to the floor. He leaned forward, his hands interlacing on the desktop.

"Mr. Wells," he said, chuckling. "Everybody wants you out of this county. *I* want you out of this county."

"I don't think it was you."

"Neither do I, but I'm keeping an open mind. The point I'm trying to make is . . ." One of his ham-hock hands dropped down behind the desk. I heard a drawer slide open. His hand came up again, carrying a copy of the local daily. He threw it down on the desk before me. "Look there."

I reached for the paper, and gasped as the pain in my chest shot up the back of my neck. I reached again, more slowly now. I opened the paper.

It was on the bottom of page one: STAR SUICIDE PIECE ON COUNTY AGENDA.

"They're trying to figure out if they can sue," said Tammany Bird.

I grimaced. "Oof," I said. "Sue me?"

"No, sue your paper. They're trying to figure out if they can lynch you."

"Great."

"Let me be the first to invite you to the meeting."

"Thanks. I don't suppose it would help if I told you I didn't write the piece."

"Nope. Folks around here are kind of simpleminded about these things. They figure if it says 'By John Wells' on it, why, it must be by John Wells."

"Ha," I said bitterly.

"Just like they figure if a fella comes up here to do a series of articles about the suicides of our children, he shouldn't oughta turn it into some sensationalistic piece of bullsquat about she says murder and police cover up and I don't know what else."

"Oh yeah," I said. "I forgot about the cover-up part. I really didn't write it, you know."

"Uh-huh."

I took another tack. "What if I told you I was beginning to think the article was true." That made his eyebrows rise. "Not the cover-up part," I said quickly. "But the murder part."

He seemed less than amused. "Go on," he said.

"Well, lookit, first someone leads me into the woods and tells me Death's out there. And I find a dog hanging from a tree—just the way they found Michelle Thayer. Then, through no fault of my own, my article comes out leading with Janet Thayer's accusation. And suddenly up pops Death himself and takes a hack at me. What do you make of all that."

"Kids."

"Come on, Chief, he was trying to kill me."

"Maybe."

"Not maybe."

"Maybe. Anyway, whether you wrote it or not, that piece cut a lot of folks nice and deep. I'm not surprised if someone got out of hand."

"What about the dog?" I said. "The story hadn't even appeared then."

Tammany Bird settled back in his chair again, mountainous. He bridged his fingers over his belly. "It struck me," he said very slowly. "It struck me that you did not write about that in your story."

I shrugged. "I had a feeling maybe Janet Thayer had arranged it. I didn't want to cause her any more grief."

"Decent of you. Do you still think that?"

"No," I said, which was the truth.

"What do you think now?"

"I haven't decided yet," I said, which was not the truth.

I could see him considering this behind his pale eyes. I could see the gears of the sharp mind in there working it over. I expected him to go on, but instead he stood up suddenly. He towered above me.

"Always a pleasure talking to you, Mr. Wells," he said.

Painfully, I worked myself into a standing position.

"Rest assured," said Tammany Bird, "that I will give this matter all the attention I think it deserves."

Somehow, this made me feel neither restful nor assured.

"Meanwhile," he went on, "may I ask if you have any plans to travel outside the county line in the near future."

"No," I said.

"Why not make some?" he suggested.

"Because," I said quietly. I gestured at the paper lying on his desk. "I have a meeting to attend."

25

The Artful Dodge had taken a beating, but it would live. The Triple A towed it to a gas station in town, and Bird had a patrol car take me up the mountain to my hotel. In the morning—late in the morning, when I heaved my stiffened corpse out of bed—I called a cab and returned to the diner for breakfast. Afterward I went to the station to hear the bad news. It was not too bad. There was no damage to the workings or the frame. The worst of it was a damaged brake drum. I also needed a new tire and some headlights.

"Should be running by this afternoon," the mechanic said. "After that, though, it's going to cost you in body work."

I laughed. "I don't even work on my body, son," I told him.

There was a pay phone at the edge of the lot. I used it to call the office.

I asked for Lansing.

"Hi, killer, what's up?" she said.

I told her.

"Oh God. How do you feel?" she said.

"Very old. Very sore."

"I hate to think Cambridge is right about this. That it's murder."

"It could be. But that won't make him right. It'll just make him look right."

"Which will prolong his tenure."

"This too shall pass, my love."

"It better. Ever since your private conference with him, he's been taking it out on McKay something awful."

"All right. Let me have it."

"Yesterday he had him assigned to cover the unveiling of a new kind of chewy candy shaped like a mouse."

I laughed. "No, really, Lansing. What'd he do?"

She was silent.

"You're not joking," I said.

"Today he's got the intrepid reporter hot on the trail of a new phone book promotion where a bunch of women dress up as yellow pages and dance and sing in Times Square."

"I knew I should have killed him. How's McKay taking it?"

"Not so good. He's got a theory about it. Says Cambridge has decided to counteract your bad influence on the staff by breaking him—McKay—and making him the relatability poster boy. A sort of Judas goat."

"Yeah. Or maybe he just likes breaking people."

"I think McKay would quit—"

". . . if he didn't have a baby. Yeah, and Cambridge knows it." There was another pause, and now I asked her: "What about you?"

I heard her let out a held breath. "He took a different tack with me," she said.

"Go on."

"Only if you promise not to play the white knight."

"He went for you."

"Last night. God damn, it was odious. He took me out to the Press Room."

"Well, well. At least he's not cheap."

"Said he wanted to discuss some story ideas with me. Then he tried to get me drunk."

I laughed. "I would like to've seen that."

"He kept ordering and ordering. Only he couldn't be too obvious about it, so he had to match me scotch for scotch."

"Poor bastard."

"At two this morning me and a bartender had to shovel him into a cab. He was singing sea chanties." She sighed. "He hasn't come in yet today."

"Lay low, Lancer."

"You're a dangerous friend to have, Mr. Wells."

"If it'll make you feel better, the county legislature up

here is holding a meeting tonight on whether or not they've got legal grounds to run me through a meat grinder."

"You're joking. You're going, I suppose."

"Have to. I'm supposed to bring the meat grinder."

"And if I told you to be careful, you'd say, 'Don't talk to me like that, Lansing.' "

"How's the Dellacroce trial?"

"Boring, unless you read the *News*."

"That's what I want to hear. See you, kid."

"Seeya."

I hung up. I called Janet Thayer. There was no answer. I now officially had nothing to do.

I spent some time wandering around town. Off the main road, past the houses with their neatly kept lawns, their swing sets, bicycles, basketball hoops. I thought about what Chandler Burke had said. People moving from the city. For their kids' sake. Fighting to preserve their houses and their lawns, their good schools, their good neighbors. And then their kids despairing around them, dying by their own hands.

Now, with the electric trains and the office parks and the bulldozers coming, even what they'd fought for would probably be gone. Changed, at least, from what it had been. There'd be more houses, a wider range of people. Harder to keep it all bright and shiny. Harder to keep it just the way you want. Maybe it would be better for the kids in the end. Maybe not.

I remembered the feeling I'd sometimes had, walking on a deserted road. I'd look at the lights in the window of a house, and it would seem warm and pleasant inside. I'd envy the family there. I'd feel left out. But I'd been inside, behind the lighted window too. It wasn't always what it seemed, wasn't always warm, wasn't always pleasant. The people of Grant County knew that now, if they hadn't known it before.

After a while I wandered over to the courthouse again and talked to Bird. I asked him if they'd made anything of the paint they'd scraped off my car.

"It's black," said Bird.

"Modern detective work is a miracle," I said.

I wandered around town some more.

At four the car was done. I paid for it on the company credit card. Then I drove back up to my hotel. I lay down for an hour to rest my weary bones. I woke up at six, had dinner at the hotel, headed down to the meeting.

It was scheduled for eight. I got there at eight-fifteen. I was hoping for a chance to sneak in the back.

The faceless, concrete county hall was alight at every window. I wondered if it was the torchlight of the angry mob inside. I parked in the lot out back. I went in through two glass doors.

It was a long walk down the hall to the meeting room. It seemed like a long walk anyway. When I got there, I stood outside the huge wooden door and listened.

I could hear the booming voice of Walter Summers. To my relief, he was not talking about me.

"I have exempted myself from this vote—just as I did when I was a member of the Z.B.A. But that doesn't mean I can't put in a word or two. As most of you know, my engineering firm played a major rôle in preparing the impact statements for the Capstandard office park. While not voting, I can assure you that the concerns of a small group of agitators are ill founded and should not stop this project from going through. . . ."

I had time to recognize the name: Capstandard. It was that gash of a place on the hill beneath my hotel. Then a voice behind me said:

"Mr. Wells?"

I turned, startled. It was Michael Summers, Walter's surviving son. Dressed in a gray suit with a port tie, he looked as handsome as any politician could wish his son to look. He had his handsome grin on, too, and it reached right into his blue eyes. He extended his hand to me. I shook it, grateful for a friendly face.

"You're a brave man, Mr. Wells," he said quietly.

I nodded. "How bad is it in there?"

He made a balancing gesture with his hand. "If it were me, I'd be walking in the opposite direction," he said. But the glint in his eyes told me differently.

"When do I come up on the agenda?"

He glanced at his watch. "You should be next. But

seriously, you can't just walk in there. The place will go crazy. Let me take you around to the legislators' entrance. They usually leave the door open. You should be able to catch the whole show." I hesitated. "Does that insult your courage?" he asked, smiling.

"On the contrary, it compliments my cowardice," I told him.

He laughed, and led me down the hall. He took me around a corner to a door with a window of pebbled glass. He tried the knob. It was locked. He went into his pants pocket and brought forth a hefty ring of keys. He unlocked the door and I followed him inside.

"It's nice to have friends in high places," he whispered.

The room we were in was a small one. Directly across from us was the other door to the meeting room, the one the legislators came through to get to their table. The door was cracked open and a shaft of light fell through it to catch a lone hat rack, empty like the autumn trees outside.

"If you position yourself there," he said, "you should get a view of the worst of it. I do it all the time."

"Okay," I whispered.

"I'll have to leave you here. I serve as my father's administrative aide." This time his grin was appealingly boyish. "Practice," he added.

I smiled, patted his shoulder. He turned to go, but paused. He fixed me with his frank gaze. "I don't want you to think I approve of what you did, of the stories your paper published," he said simply. "But I'm a good judge of character."

"That's true," I said.

"And it's an imperfect world."

"That's also true," I said.

"Well . . ."

"Thank you, son," I said. I meant it.

"Chalk it up to making peace with the press. Political savvy," he said, with another grin. "It runs in the family."

Then he turned and left the room. I heard the door click shut behind him. Alone in the semidarkness, I moved toward the shaft of light. Stepping into it, I peeked into the meeting room. I had a pretty clear view. To my left was the long curved table where the dozen members of the legislature sat.

I could only see the ends of it unless I shifted and brought myself too much into the open. To my right was the audience. They looked like one of those cheap pictures in which the artist did not want to paint all the faces in the crowd so he paints the same face over and over again. In this case the same grim, angry face.

But they were not the same. A few stood out. David Brandt was there, in the front row. He looked very pale in his dark suit, and his hair looked very red. He sat upright, staring directly before him, his hands folded in his lap. The portrait of a high school principal with a score to settle.

The Scofields, Carla and Larry, were also seated in front. They looked nervous. She had a manila folder in her hand and she kept fidgeting with it. He kept leaning over to pat her hand.

Chief Bird was there, seated by the door, looking huge. I also noticed a group of high school students sitting together near the back. Joanne and Mindy, Nancy Scofield's friends, were among them. They were sitting very quietly, observing the proceedings.

I did not see Chris Thomas or Janet Thayer. I scanned the audience more closely for them. And, as I did, I got a shock. There, seated in the back row, was Chandler Burke. Wearing a navy-blue suit buttoned high, her thin lips pressed tight enough to whiten, she looked formidable: the school-marm warrior. Maybe, I thought; maybe there'll be one strong voice raised on my behalf.

Just then a gavel whacked. A sonorous voice intoned: "Now let's move on to the matter of John Wells."

26

Hands rose in the audience at once. The voice went on: "David Brandt is the first scheduled speaker. He is, as you know, the principal of the Grant Valley High School."

Brandt stood up. His face was solemn. He went into this jacket pocket and brought out a single three-by-five index card.

"I know that the legislators have read the articles by Mr. John Wells in the *New York Star*," he said, glancing at the card. "Most of you also know that I was instrumental in giving Mr. Wells access to interviews and information that made those articles possible. For this, I feel I owe you and the entire community an apology."

My heart sank. It had not exactly been bobbing merrily along to begin with, but now it went right down to the bottom.

"The fact is, I was taken in," Brandt continued. "Taken in, and then betrayed. I can only imagine that the need for the *Star* to boost its circulation, or for Mr. Wells to enhance his reputation, or both, superseded the requirements of ethical journalism. And most other ethical considerations as well. In any case, because of my cooperation with Mr. Wells and the *Star*, our community, our county, our high school, our police force—all of us—have been libeled. I have written a strong letter to the newspaper, and I ask the legislature to do the same. I have also had a few private discussions with attorneys, and I wish to strongly recommend legal action on an individual and a community level." He sat down.

Carla Scofield was next. Her husband stood next to her. She clutched his arm for support. Her hands trembling violently, she opened her manila folder and removed a copy of the article about their daughter. The manila folder slipped from her grasp, slid to the floor. Larry stooped to retrieve it.

But Mrs. Scofield was already speaking, holding the article before her. "Reading this," she said in a trembling voice, "I felt as if my daughter had died all over again—"

Which was as far as she could get. She broke down, sobbing into her husband's shoulder.

"Oof," I said from my post behind the door.

"Mr. Executive," Larry Scofield said, "my wife can't continue just now . . . if we could . . . maybe later . . ."

"Of course," intoned the executive. "We understand."

"Oof, oof, oof," I said.

And on it went. Chief Bird got up and assured the community that every one of the tragedies of the last few weeks had been thoroughly investigated. The executive assured him that that assurance was unnecessary. The crowd assured them both with a round of applause. Some students stood up and suggested various adolescent means of revenge on my poor person. Tar and feathering was one I remember. And that was the comic relief.

Finally, Chandler stood up. I allowed myself a small glimmer of hope: maybe she would defend me. Then I got a good look at the expression on her face, and the glimmer went out.

"My name is Chandler Burke," she said softly. "I run a phone hotline for the depressed in Brentford, Connecticut. Mr. Wells visited me there yesterday. I hadn't, at that point, seen the articles he wrote. Like Mr. Brandt, I trusted Mr. Wells. I had worked with him once before, and he had shown himself to be an able and honest reporter. Now that I've read the *Star* series, I understand that he was playing on our past association—and on my ignorance of what he was up to—to continue his so-called investigation into these events. When I heard about this meeting, I felt it my duty to come here and warn you that Mr. Wells is still on the warpath, as you might say. He's still looking for proof that Michelle Thayer was murdered." She began to sit down, smoothing her skirt behind in preparation. But she rose again, raising a finger.

"Yes, Miss Burke," said the executive.

"I'd also like to say that I would be more than willing to

participate as a witness in any legal action the legislature decides to take."

"Thank you, Miss Burke."

"Thanks a lot," I muttered.

She sat, but there was plenty more where that came from. The meeting had become an open discussion on everything from my ethics to my prose style to my parentage. Finally, slowly, the talk wound down. The matter appeared to be headed for a committee. Deadlines for legal action would be examined and so on. The discussion was over.

At this point I briefly considered stepping out of my hiding place and making an attempt to explain. It was Chandler's speech, in fact, that stopped me. She was right. For better or for worse, I was working Cambridge's angle now. I was looking into the possibility that a suicide had been a homicide. I didn't think I'd get a chance to explain much more than that before an ugly mob scene erupted, with me at the center.

Instead I reminded myself that discretion is the better part of valor. Valorously, I crept from my hiding place, slinked down the hall, and escaped into the night.

27

I got in my car, but I did not drive away. I needed a minute. Public evisceration takes it out of you. I sat there in the dark for a while, smoking a cigarette. Then I got my keys out and put them in the ignition. But as I reached for them, the doors of the county hall opened and the people began filing out. The work of the good folks of Grant Valley was done for the evening.

I sat back. I watched them. I thought nasty thoughts. I listened to the sound of car doors opening and closing. I saw headlights going on all over the lot. I heard engines roaring.

I glanced up and saw Chandler Burke. She was striding purposefully away from the lot. I could not hear her low heels rapping the asphalt, but I could imagine the swift, unforgiving sound they made. She reached the sidewalk and turned right. She disappeared around a corner of the building.

I hit the ignition. The engine turned over. My brand-new headlights came on. I threw the car into reverse, backed out of my parking space. I joined the line of cars moving toward the street.

I went right, after Chandler. I found her at a bus stop on Main Street. I remembered Chris Thomas had told me that Michelle took a bus to Brentford. I pulled the Artful Dodge over to the curb. I began to roll down the window. The mechanism had been damaged when the car went off the road, and I had to muscle the crank around. As I did, Chandler saw me. She looked this way and that, as if for help. By that time I had the window open.

"Get in," I said. "Let's talk."

"There's nothing to talk about," she told me. Her voice

sounded the way I figured her heels had sounded on the pavement: clipped, hard.

"Yeah, I heard your speech."

She seemed surprised. But she recovered quickly. "If you don't leave me alone," she said, "I'll call for help."

"The cops would love that."

"Then just go away."

"I think you ought to give me a chance to explain," I said. "It isn't like you not to listen."

That was good: that got her. I saw her hesitate. I pressed the point.

"There's another side to this," I said out the window. "Let me give you a lift home. Let me say my piece. I hear there aren't many buses around anyway."

For another few seconds she weighed her anger against her sense of fairness. Her fairness won out, which is how I'd figured it.

"All right," she said brusquely. She stepped forward, reached for the door handle, and pulled. The door didn't open. "Well, unlock it," she snapped.

"It is unlocked. It must've gotten busted last night."

I got out of the car and waited till she came around to my side. As she went by me, she threw her head back, her nose in the air. I caught the scent of her hair, her shampoo. Then she ducked down into the car. I went after her.

I edged from the curb into the Main Street traffic: the ten or fifteen cars still pulling away from the county hall.

"It's a twenty-minute drive," she said primly. "I'd start talking if I were you."

"Your concern touches me," I said. I'd had enough. "So does your civic mindedness, come to think of it. 'I'll be happy to serve as a witness in a suit against Mr. Wells.' Thanks a lot, sister."

"I'm not your sister."

"Thank God for small favors," I said. "What the hell's wrong with you anyway, lady? You could've called and talked to me about it. I hope this isn't the way you run your god-damned hotline."

"You're being abusive and obscene," she said.

I had an answer to that, but I set it aside. She crossed

her arms beneath her breasts. I drove in silence. We pulled out of town and onto the long road to Brentford.

It was a crystal clear night. Cool, beautiful. The stars were out full force. Before me, the road was still clear. No night mist had risen.

I stole a glance at Chandler's unlovely profile. She turned on me.

"What can there be to say?" she said, leaning forward. "I read your piece. It was cruel and it was sensationalistic. How could you, John?"

"I didn't."

"Oh, what's that supposed to mean?"

"It means I didn't write the thing."

"It has your name on it."

"My editor got hold of it. He rewrote every word."

That stopped her a second. But it wasn't going to be that easy. She plopped back against her seat, arms crossed.

"Still," she said.

"Still what?"

"Still—I don't know. You could've withdrawn your name."

"I never saw it, Chandler. I read it in the paper just like everybody else."

Again she paused. The road beneath my tires grew narrow now and pitted. The town was gone. The houses were fewer and farther between. Soon the woods closed in and the road began to twist and roll between the trees.

"Listen—" I said.

"You're driving too fast," said Chandler.

I slowed down.

"So why did you come to the church?" she said. "Why did you ask me all those questions about Michelle."

"I'm trying to find out if she was murdered."

She let out an exasperated, "Oh!"

"If she wasn't, the editor will print a page-three apology. If she was . . . well, then we'll have the truth."

"I never heard such nonsense in my life."

More silence. More driving. The road wound deep into the woods. It was dark on every side of us, for the most part. Now and then the gold light of a window shone amid the trees.

"Someone tried to kill me last night," I said.

She turned quickly, concerned. She turned away just as fast.

"Something's going on up here, Chandler. Three kids are dead. I want to know why."

She still had nothing to say. Annoyed, I took out a cigarette, jabbed it between my lips.

"I don't like the smoke," she said.

"It'll go out the window."

"It's not good for you. They won't have to kill you if you keep that up."

I threw the thing out the window, unlit.

"Damn it," I said. "I didn't write that story, Chandler. Don't you know me better than that?"

Now she took one long look at me. Even in the darkness, I saw her eyes shine. When she turned away this time, she turned full away, to the window. She stared out, saying nothing.

And the road wound through the crystal night. And the trees hovered in silhouette against the sky, and the stars shone through them. We went past the old church where her hotline was. We went into town. Past houses first, then into a quaint New England city center.

"Turn here," she said. She spoke very softly.

I guided the car off the main drag. We went past a row of streetlamps. They lay halos of light down on neat little lawns. Back on the lawns sat a number of red-brick apartment buildings, all the same.

Chandler Burke pointed to one of them. "This is it."

I pulled over to the curb. Stopped. Without a word she yanked at the door handle. It stuck.

"Oh damn!" I heard her whisper.

The handle snapped. The door swung open. She got out.

For a second I sat behind the wheel, watching her go up the walk. The Dodge's engine idled. Its lights peered aimlessly into the night.

Then I killed the lights, the engine. I got out of the car and went after her.

I followed her up the concrete path. I heard her heels clicking in front of me. She didn't turn. She came to the brick building and paused as she unlocked the front door. She disappeared inside. I followed, caught the door before it shut. Went in after her.

I saw her going up the stairway. I went up too. I saw her skirt flicking around the banister on the second-floor landing. When I reached the landing, she was standing in the hall before an apartment door. She was fighting to get her key in the lock. She couldn't do it. She was too upset. I stepped forward, took her keys from her. She stood by, pale and frowning, while I opened the door for her.

She went into the room before me, snapped on the light. I stepped in. We were in the living room. It was neat, drab, and dim. Colorless sofas, chairs, and bookshelves stood against the white walls. Faded pictures hung on them. An orange-and-white cat, curled on an easy chair, lifted its head. "Meow," it said and thumped off the chair onto the floor and padded forward. It wound itself around Chandler's ankles.

"Know you?" she said. Her voice was still soft, but it went through me. "I haven't seen you in almost twenty years, John. How on earth could I know you?"

I came toward her. Her lips were tight. Her hands folded and unfolded on her coat.

"It had to be this way, Chandler. You know that."

The anger flared in her eyes like embers in the wind. "I know nothing like that. It didn't have to be this way at all. Know you!" And now the anger glittered behind tears. I couldn't look. I turned away. "Don't do that!" she snapped. "The last time I saw you, you did that. You turned away from me."

I stared at the floor. "I was married," I muttered.

"To a cruel, selfish, nasty little rich girl who didn't even—" She bit back the rest of it. "And you had a daughter then. And you had something about you, about the way you were . . ."

I raised my head and nodded. "Yeah. Well, now my daughter's dead."

"That's not it!" she cried. "That's not it at all. It isn't that she's dead." She was trembling all over. "It's that you are. I saw it the minute I recognized you in the church. Empty . . . Trying not to look up from your work . . . I hate to see it. Why do I have to see it? What is it to me? Why don't you go away? I have my own—"

So I stepped forward and kissed her. I guess I did it just to prove her wrong, just to show her there was still some life left in me. I don't know why I did it. And then it didn't matter much why. I had her shoulders in my hands, and her hands were moving, fevered, on my face and neck. I had my lips pressed to hers and her lips were parting for me and our tongues were hot together. Even through her coat I felt how warm her body was, and soft. I felt that surprising eagerness, that hunger, that I remembered from long ago. We strained to be closer to each other, and closer still.

Then we pulled away. We looked into each other's faces—the haggard and saddened faces that we'd earned.

"Long time no see," I said.

"Yes," she whispered.

And we were together again.

28

For a long time we said nothing. A sweet time that was not like time at all. Nothing moved or changed in it but us, and our bodies together. And when we lay still in each other's arms, naked on the naked bed, I thought I could feel the great darkness motionless all around us.

Her body was as warm as I had thought it would be. She lay with it pressed along the length of mine. Her head was on my chest. I smelled her hair.

"You know," she murmured, "I really wonder . . ."

"Don't," I said. I kissed her hair gently.

"You feel so good."

"You too."

"I just wonder, that's all. About all that time . . ." She raised her face to me. I kissed her. "It makes me sad."

"Chandler—"

"Ssh. Let me." She lay her cheek against my chest again. "Everything is also what it might have been, that's all. That's all I'm saying. . . ."

"No," I said. "A thing is only what it is. I'm sure of it."

She took a long breath, let it out in a sigh. I trailed my fingers up her back. She whispered: "Why didn't you?. . . Ever call me, come to see me? Try to find me? When it was over with Constance."

"It just wasn't that way," I said. "It took a while before it ended, and then, I don't know, I was other places. There were other people." After a moment I asked her: "Why? I mean, did you? . . ."

"Pine away and die for you?" I didn't answer. She said: "No. Well. I pined away. I nearly died. But not for you."

"Has it been that tough?"

"Not really. Not all of it. Most of the time my work has been satisfying. There hasn't been much else. A few . . . relationships along the way. Not much. Or, at least, after a while it didn't seem like much to me." She pressed even closer. "My parents died a while back. About ten years ago. First my father had a heart attack. Then my mother. She took a long time to go. I was very close to both of them, Mom especially. Too close, I imagine. And one night . . . not long after she died . . . One night, I was in my room in White Plains. Making dinner. And I turned on the gas—and the flame didn't catch. And I just stood there. With the gas on."

I closed my eyes, my lips against her brow.

"It made me feel . . . woozy," she said. "The gas, I mean. Like all the blood was rushing to my head." She rubbed her face against my chest. Very softly, she murmured: "Then I turned it off. Called up a friend of mine. She worked at a clinic nearby."

I didn't say anything. I had nothing to say.

Now, Chandler moved away from me. Rolled over on her back, her head resting on my arm. She stared blankly at the ceiling in the dark.

"And you?" she asked.

"Oh. You know. The work," I said.

"The work."

"Yeah. I've been at the *Star* almost . . . Jesus, it'll be ten years, I guess, pretty soon. They hired me out of White Plains after I did this series on the mob there . . ."

"The one where they blew up your car."

"You heard about that, huh?"

"It was pretty big news."

"Yeah, well . . . A lot of indictments came out of the thing, you know, so the *Star* called me." I put my free hand behind my head. Lay beside her, sort of gazing up at nothing like she was. "That's what I wanted. To be in New York and all."

"You sound . . . regretful."

I considered. "No. They've been pretty good to me, for the most part. I do pretty much as I please, cover what I want. It's a good paper, too, no matter what the management tries to do to it. You know, they'd put the funnies on the front page if they could get away with it. But the staff's good, the reporters, the people. That's what matters, what makes it good." I shrugged a little. "I've gotten offers. A couple magazines. L.A. was after me for a while. And every year, the *Star* asks me if I want to be an editor. I don't know. I've thought about doing a column recently, but . . . I don't know . . . I like the beat. I like what I do."

A few seconds of silence passed between us. Then Chandler said: "I ask you how you've been, and you tell me about your job." I kept quiet. "Well?"

"Well, what?"

"Well, what about the rest of it?"

"For the rest of it . . ." I told her. "For the rest of it, I got by."

She turned to me. "And when your daughter died?"

"Still. I got by."

She smiled a little. "Somehow, that's what I thought you'd say."

"It was a long time ago, Chandler."

I felt her lay her palm very softly against my cheek. I leaned against the coolness of it. "What can I give you, John?" she said.

"Nothing. You don't have to give me anything."

She withdrew her hand. "She talked to them, you know. Michelle."

I shifted. "What?"

"To Nancy Scofield and Fred Summers. She had a number of conversations with them on the hotline. She talked with both of them before they died."

I didn't answer. Chandler lifted off my arm. She propped herself up on a pillow. I reached for my shirt where it lay on the floor and wrestled a cigarette from the pocket. Leaned back, lit it. Chandler eyed me, but she let it go.

"I just wanted to tell you," she said. "I just wanted to give you that."

"I understand." I smoked, waited for her to go on.

"All the conversations are confidential," she said after a while. "We keep records, but they aren't detailed at all. Just a first name, usually, maybe a note or two on an index card. They're mostly for statistical purposes: for grant proposals and things like that. Anyway, after Michelle died, I got curious and went through them, looking to see if she'd spoken to any of the others. I found Fred and Nancy both. On Fred's card she'd written 'Family problems.' After Nancy's name she'd written the word 'Love'."

"And you're sure they were the same kids?"

"Yes. She marked the date down when they died."

I considered it. "Do you think their deaths may have pushed her over the edge?"

"I think . . . it's possible," Chandler said slowly. "I mean, she never even told me about them. She never mentioned them to me. That wasn't like her at all."

I thought about Chris Thomas. I thought about him and Michelle meeting in the woods, talking in the woods. *She told me everything*, he'd said. Had she discussed the suicides of her hotline clients with him?

Beside me Chandler Burke shifted, rolled over onto her side. She closed her eyes.

"I wanted to give you that," she said again.

I glanced over at the bedside table. My watch was there, the dial glowing. It was after two A.M.

"John?" Chandler's voice was growing dim, sleepy.

"Yeah," I said.

"I'm glad."

I nodded. "Yeah," I said.

"I'm very glad," she said.

In another moment her breath came long and even. She was asleep.

29

I didn't stay. I wanted to. Almost did. The prospect of the morning almost held me there. The warmth of her, the gentleness again after sleeping. Her slow, speculative approach to pleasure. I could guess they would be something to wake up to. Something new under the sun. But I didn't stay. The thing was working in me now. I had to move. I had to think it out.

I got out of bed and dressed quietly. I left her a note. Never mind what it said. I kissed her while she slept, and left.

I drove back to Grant Valley slowly. The roads had remained clear. The stars were still shining. The forests at the roadside seemed mysterious, like no one had ever seen them at this hour but me. The moon was down. The darkness was complete.

The center of town was nearly as dark. The unlighted windows of the stores and offices reflected nothing. Only the streetlamps broke the night. I passed on under them, toward the hills.

I came to the old graveyard at the bottom of the hotel's mountain. The skewed, time-washed stones shone in my headlights for a moment, then faded back into the night. I passed on. I saw the Capstandard office park on the mountain's other side. My mind flashed back to last night's meeting. The thought made me shiver. I went up the hill.

There were no lights on at the hotel. When I came into the parking lot and switched off the engine, the night dropped over me like a curtain. I got out and tentatively made my way toward my room.

I got about halfway down the slate path and stopped

dead. I stood there—frozen—for several long moments. There was a scrabbling sound in the darkness ahead of me. It was coming from my door. I squinted toward the sound. I couldn't see a thing.

Now, I edged forward. A cool breeze came up the mountain and, in the forest to my left, the empty branches rattled. I stopped again to listen. I told myself that that was all I'd heard. But the breeze died, and the other sound continued. A rattling sound. Someone was working the doorknob.

I took another step, and I knew that Death was there—or whoever it was who'd decided to play the part. I saw his silhouette dimly against the pale door. His white skull mask glowed in the starlight. He was trying to get into my room.

I didn't think. I just went for him. It was a bad move. I must've had twenty yards to cover. About halfway there a stick snapped under my shoe.

I saw Death spin around. I stopped, waiting for him to charge me. There was a long moment when we both stood still, staring at each other through the depths of the darkness.

Then, silently, he bolted.

I never really had a chance to catch him. He was strong and fast. He darted around the building and off into the woods. I ran after him as best I could, but I was no match for him at all.

He went down the far side of the mountain. I trotted behind, losing ground with every step. I plunged into the night woods. Among the trees the dark grew thicker still. For a while I could see the glowing white skull vanishing and reappearing between the trunks. Once, he glanced back at me, but he did not slow his pace. My ears filled with the sound of my own breathing. My chest hurt as I fought for air. But the steep incline carried me forward. I kept going, even when I knew he'd as good as gotten away.

Finally, as the ground evened out toward the hill's base, I lost him completely. I saw him faintly for another instant, still moving as quickly as before. Then the night just seemed to swallow him. He was gone. Maybe if I'd kept running, I'd have caught sight of him again. But my cigarette-battered wind had finally given out, and I could see it was hopeless.

I stood still. The forest had opened up before me. The

moaning trees still clustered at my back, but in front of me there were only a few of them. In the place of the waving branches, of the still, silhouetted trunks, I saw dim gray shapes rising from the earth like ghosts. I had come down into the graveyard.

I turned and looked back over my shoulder. It was a long trek back up the hill. I leaned over and put my hands on my knees. I drew deep breaths trying to recover. I thought about the Dellacroce trial, about how pleasant it would've been just then to be seated in a warm, well-lighted courtroom, scribbling endless notes on endless pads. I straightened. I could see the black ribbon of the road beyond the cemetery's edge. I decided to walk down to it and hike back up to the hotel on solid pavement.

I came down among the graves. They leaned this way and that, gray and faceless. The night seemed solemn as I moved among them.

I walked toward the road. I caught sight of a white figure in the corner of my vision. I spun. I saw the statue of an angel, bent in silent mourning. The sight of her sent a chill up my spine.

I heard something. Something in the grass. I looked down. I was standing beside a hip-high monument. Faintly, I could make out the words chiseled on it: I could see where the name was, and the dates of birth and death beneath. Nothing else. I shook my head, annoyed with myself.

And then a clay-encrusted hand shot out of the earth, grabbed my ankle, and held on fast.

30

I screamed like hell. I was terrified. I yanked my foot back hard. The hand stretched out of the grave. It held on. I cursed, desperate. I yanked again. This time my leg came free. I stumbled back with the force of the reaction. I reached behind me blindly. My fingers found the cold, slippery stone above another grave. I clutched it. It kept me on my feet.

Now I stood petrified, staring, as a second hand clawed its way free of the earth. My mind kept screaming, *It's him! It's him!* as I fought to regain my senses.

I peered through the dark. The two hands clutched the ground. They were pulling their way up. A head came into view. I wanted to run, to get the hell out of there. But I battled the urge. *Whatever it is*, I told myself, *it can only be human. Human is all there is.*

And it was. It was human, all right. Now the head came clear of the ground. White in the blackness, the sweating, bewildered young face of Chris Thomas appeared.

He gasped with the effort of pulling himself up. "Give me a hand, for God's sake, will you, Wells," he said.

It took another moment before I could register what I saw. But that was all it took to dispel the fear. In its place, almost at once, came red fury. I reached down and grabbed the idiot by the lapels.

"I'll give you a bloody hand," I said. And I dragged him roughly out of the hole. It was hidden in the grass, that hole, but already I'd figured out what it was: another entrance to the limestone caves that networked the mountain's underground.

I yanked the punk to his feet. Maybe he was on his feet.

Maybe I had him a couple inches off the ground, I'm not sure.

"You!" I shouted into his nose. "What the hell's wrong with you?"

A lopsided grin split the pale, boyish face idiotically. "Uh . . ." he said.

"Listen, Creature Features," I said. "I've been dragged out of bed to meet a hanging dog, I've been run off the road and chased with a tire iron. My reputation is shot and my body hurts all over. I'm in a bad mood, so talk to me before I put you back in that grave for good."

"I . . . I . . . I . . ." said Chris Thomas.

"Punk!" I swung him around till his legs slammed into the gravestone behind me.

"Ow! Shit, Wells!" he remarked.

"Where is it?"

"Wha . . ."

"The skull mask. Is it down in the cave?"

His eyes widened. "I don't have—" I jolted him, banged him against the stone again. He said "Ow!" again.

"Why'd you kill the dog, Dracula?"

"I didn't," he cried. "I swear."

I banged him back yet again. "Oh, my mood is worsening, friend. I went down into the caves that night. I found the paper you burned down there. It was the same paper Michelle drew her pictures on. I thought maybe it belonged to Janet Thayer. But it was something Michelle gave to you."

Thomas started to cry. His whole face crumpled, the features collapsing into each other. He squeaked as he cried: eee, eee, eee. I'd had enough of him, and anyway my arms were tired. I hurled him down onto the ground. He lay there sprawled beneath the gravestone, crying.

"Did you kill her?" I said. But I knew the answer to that already.

Thomas shook his head, crying. "No," he said. Eee, eee, eee.

"Do you know who did?"

He wiped his nose with his sleeve. "Death," he said.

"Christ." I needed time to calm down. I was ready to kick the bugger's head in.

I put my hands on my hips and took a few deep breaths.
I paced a step or two to the right of him, turned, and paced
a step or two to his left. Then I stood over him, looking down.
He straightened, afraid. He was now half sitting, his head
resting against the stone.

"You watch too many horror movies," I said, as calmly
as I could.

He nodded, snuffling. "I know that," he said sullenly.

"Don't you have parents or something?"

"Just my mother. She works at night."

"Right." I gestured at him. "Stop crying."

"I didn't kill her," he said. "I loved her. It was him."

"Death."

He nodded again.

"All right. All right." I went into my pocket, pulled out
a cigarette. Torched it, squinting at the sudden light of the
match. The smoke went in hard, but I took it. At least if it
killed me now, I wouldn't have far to go. "Let's hear everything," I said.

Still snuffling, still wiping at his nose, Chris Thomas
struggled to sit up on the grave. I listened awhile as he fought
to control himself. Then he said: "I saw him. I saw him in
the woods. I saw him watching us—me and Michelle—when
we talked together at the root cellar. The last two days, I
looked down into the woods, and I saw him standing there.
We talked about death a lot. All the time. I knew he'd come
for us in the woods."

I snorted smoke. "Not death," I said. "A person. A
person in a skull mask." But I remembered my first sight of
him near Janet Thayer's house. A tough sight to take for a
mixed-up guy like Chris.

He put his hands to his head and moaned. "Oh God, I
don't know, I don't know," he said. "That's what Michelle
told me. She told me it was someone in a mask. And then
she was dead. A week later she was dead, and I just don't
know anymore."

"Okay, okay," I said quietly. "What happened then."

"When . . . when she was gone . . . I went looking for
him. . . . In the woods everyday. I wanted . . . I wanted him
to take me too."

"Oh great."

"But he wouldn't come. He wasn't there. He wouldn't . . ." He moved his hands to cover his face. "I'm so confused. I'm so fucking confused all the time."

I sighed, feeling guilty. "It's all right, son," I said. "We're gonna figure it out."

"That's what I thought. I thought, when you came, when Mr. Brandt introduced you to everyone, you looked . . . I don't know, you looked like someone who knew . . . about death . . . you looked . . . like someone who could figure it out."

"So you found out where I was, and came up to the hotel to see me."

He nodded. "I traveled in the caves. I didn't want him to find me at the last minute." I heard him take a shaky breath. "But he did. I came out. I came out of the caves and saw him. He was . . . he had Sosh. The school dog. It was dead in his arms and he was . . ."

He told me. I felt a chill in the pit of my stomach. It was the first real glimpse I'd had of him: of the person who was Death. And what I glimpsed scared me. I saw the shadow of a deranged mind. Like Chris, he must have heard about me. Like Chris, he must have had something to tell me. Maybe he told himself he was hanging the dog up as a joke or a warning. But I sensed it wasn't really that: it was a kind of confession. Whether he'd actually killed Michelle or not, he must've felt responsible for it. He must've wanted someone to know that. That also must've been why he kept coming after me. If he hadn't, I probably would've dropped the story. But somewhere inside his head, I don't think he wanted me to. Part of him wanted me to find him. The other part, I suspected, wanted me very dead.

"Okay," I said when Chris was finished.

"Just like he did with Michelle, just like he made her do."

"What then?"

"I snuck by him. It was dark. I snuck by him and ran up to your place. I saw you at the window and I . . . I wanted you to see, to see he was real."

"Why didn't you knock on the bloody door?"

"I don't . . . I was afraid. . . ."

"Okay. So you led me down into the woods to find the dog, to tell me death was down there."

He nodded.

"And what about tonight?"

He looked up at me. It was a miserable look, begging me to understand. I don't know why the hell he thought I would, but he did. So I tried. "I've been waiting for him," he said. "Watching. I knew he'd come back to your place. I knew it. I saw him tonight. I saw him try to break into your place. Then you came. I went down in the caves because it was faster. I thought I could help you, that's all. I was trying to help."

I sighed again. "You were trying to help."

"I just fuck up everything."

"Forget it. I'm sorry I roughed you up. You nearly gave me a heart attack. I'm not a young man anymore, you know."

He almost smiled.

"Can you drive?" I asked him. He shook his head. "Well, then, we better start walking."

"I have my bike," he offered.

"A bike."

"A motorbike," he said. "It'll carry us."

My kidneys hurt already. "Terrific," I said. "Let's go back up the hill."

31

It beat walking. We plugged and putted up the mountain, back to the hotel.

In my room Chris sat wearily on the edge of the bed, his shoulders hunched forward, his head hung down. I sat at the desk chair, my arm draped over the back, a cigarette burning between the fingers of one hand, a glass of scotch wrapped up in the other.

After a long silence he said softly, "I feel like I've been in a nightmare."

I didn't answer. I listened. I figured I owed him that.

"I thought he was real . . . I thought he . . . Oh God, I just feel like . . . everything's so . . ." His face contorted with pain. "What am I here for? Why am I still here when she's gone?"

"Hell, that's no way to talk," I said. But I felt the question shoot into me, deep into the recesses of my brain. It hurt. "You don't decide who lives and dies. They've probably got a committee that does that somewhere."

"Well, it's a stinking committee," he told me.

"Most committees are."

"I just can't find the way," he said. His eyes were swimming. His lips were swollen with crying. He looked about five years old. "I just can't find the way to go on, Mr. Wells. You ever feel like that?" He looked up at me.

"Yeah," I said. "I've felt that way."

He looked surprised. "You have?"

"Sure I have," I said. I knew I should have said more, but I didn't. I wished Chandler was there.

The moment passed. He went on. "She used to tell me how death was beautiful, how you became part of everything, how there weren't any problems anymore, and she wouldn't have to look at her mother and know she was disappointing her. Lying to her and all." A thought passed through his mind. It made him smile bitterly. "It's like with my mother. Only with her it's the guilt."

"She on you a lot, is she?"

"Huh? Oh. No, not my guilt. Hers. The way she looks at me all the time like she's . . . so . . . sorry. You know?"

I shook my head, tried to keep him going. "Not exactly."

"Oh, just . . . You know, my dad died when I was real little, and she had to work and I came home alone and all." His smile was more like a grimace now. "I used to get scared there in the house by myself. I'd just climb into the closet and hide there till she got back. In the dark. Wishing Dad would . . . you know . . . come back." He clasped his hands together where they dangled between his knees. "She used to come home and find me there, and she'd just look at me, you know. Like she was . . . just . . . so . . . sorry. It's, like, a lot to take. Unscrews your head. And, I mean, she still looks at me like that. Sometimes I think she does this word processing stuff just so's she can work at night. So she won't have to see me. So she won't have to feel . . . sorry all the time."

I tried to think of something reassuring to say. I couldn't. Sounded crummy to me too.

He was quiet for a minute. Then: "So we talked about dying."

"Hell," I said lamely. "That's no answer."

"Oh yeah?" He raised his head. His eyes flashed angrily. "You wanna tell me what the answer is?"

The buried hurt stirred again. I fiddled with my cigarette. Changed the subject. "So you two really talked a lot?"

The anger subsided. His shoulders straightened proudly. "I told you. She told me everything. We told each other everything."

I took a sip of scotch. I took a drag on the cigarette. "Everything," I said.

"Oh yeah. Oh yeah," he said, half smiling. "We just talked and talked."

I leaned forward in my chair. "Chris," I said. "Did you

ever talk about the hotline? About the conversations she had with people on the hotline?"

He snorted. "Oh yeah. Hell yeah. Some of that stuff was pretty gritty too."

"Yeah?"

"Oh yeah."

"Did she ever mention the fact that she talked to Fred Summers and Nancy Scofield before they committed suicide?"

His lips parted. "How'd you know that?"

"Did she?"

"Yeah . . . Yeah, she was pretty upset about it."

"You think that might be the reason she killed herself?"

He considered it. "I don't know. No. I don't think so. I mean, we talked about it a long time, you know. And she seemed to get her mind right on it. She felt . . . see, at first she felt like it was her fault, like she failed them somehow. I told her, though . . . I told her, you know, I mean: they had their own problems. It seemed really to cheer her up after a while."

I studied his earnest face. "What were their problems? Fred and Nancy? Did she tell you?"

"Well, yeah, some of it." He ran his hand up through his crewcut. My eyes were fixed on him firmly now. "Nancy, I remember, Michelle said something about how she was screwing around with one of her teachers or something, and then—"

"Wait, wait a minute," I said. I had gotten to my feet. I lay down my scotch glass on the table. I snuffed the nail. I paced in front of him. "That could be it right there. I mean, she had all these secrets. Michelle. Nancy calls her up and tells her she's sleeping with a teacher. Nancy's fifteen years old: it could cost the guy his job, his career. He could even go to jail for it. Maybe he found out Michelle knew. . . ." I stopped pacing. "Who was it? Do you remember?"

He searched around in his mind for it. "No, she never told me. I mean, I'd remember something like that if she did. I mean, you know, a teacher, man. She said she couldn't tell me that 'cause he was still alive and all."

I let my breath out. "Sure. Sure." I rubbed my eyes.

Through the picture window I could see the black sky turning violet. The stars were fading. It was past five A.M.

I walked over to the desk. I pawed through the papers splattered around my typewriter there. I pulled out the notebook in which I'd copied Nancy's poem, called "A Valentine." I handed it to Chris. "I used this in my piece," I said. "It got cut out."

He looked at the page, squinting to make out my handwriting. He murmured the first lines, " 'Do you consider that I have not seen,/day after day, your moving away from me?' " He read on awhile in silence, then he handed it back to me. "I learned about Edgar Allan Poe in English. I love his stuff."

"That doesn't exactly surprise me about you, pal. Nancy liked him too." I glanced up at him. "Did Michelle tell you that?"

"No, but he wrote a poem called 'A Valentine' too. It sounded like this one . . . I don't know, kinda stilted, you know." He pointed at the notebook still in my hand. "That's 'cause he had to arrange the words to spell out the name of the person he was writing to."

"What?"

"Yeah. It was kinda like a . . . whatchamacallit."

"A cryptogram. How did it work?"

He shrugged. "I dunno. I can't remember."

I grabbed the phone, dialed McKay. It rang once, and he answered.

"Who the hell is this?" he said.

"Wells, buddy. Sorry to wake you up."

"You didn't goddamn wake me up. This goddamn baby woke me up. What the hell do you want, anyway?" I could hear the baby squawling in the background.

"Listen, daddy-o," I said.

"Shut up," said McKay.

"Go to one of your many bookshelves and pull forth your dust-encrusted volume of Edgar Allan Poe."

"All right, God damn it, just hold on."

I held on. The baby's screaming faded. I waited. The baby's screaming returned. So did McKay.

"Yeah, so what?" he said.

"Find a poem called 'A Valentine.' "

I waited. "All right," he barked at me.

"It's supposed to be, like, a code or something. . . ."

"Yeah, it's a cryptogram. There's a footnote. It says you figure it out by taking the first letter of the first line, the second letter of the second line, and so on."

"Night, dads."

"Fuck you."

I hung up. I set to work decoding the poem.

Then I said: "I'll be damned."

David Brandt.

32

I didn't get much sleep after Chris went home. By nine-thirty I was standing in front of the high school. I stood on the sidewalk, smoking a cigarette, huddled inside my overcoat. The sky had gone gray as granite and the wind had turned bitter cold.

In about five minutes a patrol car pulled up to the curb. Tammany Bird unfolded himself from within. His egg-shaped head hovered in the sky above me. He cast a pale glance down my way with his pale eyes.

"All right," he said softly. "But if it's no good, you got a date with the county line."

I nodded. We headed up the walk toward the school.

Bird was greeted with smiles in the office. I sort of hung back behind him. Brandt wasn't there. He was holding another assembly. The subject this time was the abuse of journalism. A sort of update on the meeting of the night before. I figured we could get there just in time for me to act as a diagram. I went after Bird as he strode down the hall to the auditorium.

The kids' faces turned to us as we came in the back door. Bird's khaki uniform held their attention a moment. Then they saw me. At once they began murmuring to each other. But Brandt called their eyes back to the front.

He was standing at the podium on the stage. He was wearing another of his snazzy dark suits, the ones that made his face seem whiter and his hair even more red.

"All right now, everyone," he said. His voice exuded sincerity. "Quiet down."

He waited another moment while the murmuring slowly

died. After glancing down at his notes, he took up where he'd left off.

"This is a private meeting, but I can't help feeling it would be a good thing if one of our visitors also heard what I have to say." He cleared his throat. "What I've been trying to stress so far is that I know how many of you feel about this. How terrible you feel. I feel terrible too. I want to assure you that the responsibility for what has happened is not yours. You did nothing wrong. The fault lies partially with me. But primarily it lies with a newspaper—and a newspaperman— that served the profit motive above the truth.

"Now, before I go into more detail about last night's meeting—and also suggest some actions we might take as a school—I want to show you some examples of the way in which some of the modern media have abused their freedoms."

He leaned back from his podium and glanced underneath, looking for the materials. He held up a finger. "Just a minute," he said. He walked off the stage into the wings.

The students sitting in the auditorium waited. I could almost feel their desire to turn and look at me. At first they restrained themselves. But as the moments passed, I saw the white flash of one face, then another, then another, glancing back. The murmuring began again. The students leaned toward each other. They cupped their hands before their mouths and whispered into each other's ears. The stage remained empty. The murmuring grew louder. The stage remained empty still.

Beside me I heard Chief Bird murmur, "What the hell?"

He turned to me. I shook my head.

"What the hell?" said Tammany Bird, and he started down the aisle toward the stage.

I followed. His long legs carried him quickly. I had to walk fast to keep up. My body—stiff and sore and weary— complained at the effort.

Bird reached the stage and went up the stairs. A curtain hung to the right of the podium. He pushed it aside, went through. I was right behind him.

We came into the wings: a dimly lit space. There was no one there. Various shapeless objects lay slung on the floor.

Ropes and wires and lights hung on the walls and from the ceiling above us. But that was all we saw. That and—a few steps in front of us—a heavy, gray metal fire door.

"What the bleeding hell?" said Tammany Bird. We went for the door. Bird threw his massive weight against it. It opened with a loud snap.

We came out onto the edge of the school playing field: a long expanse of grass that rolled up from a dip to meet the sidewalk at the side of the school. We saw David Brandt. He was just cresting the rise of the hill. He reached the sidewalk. He began walking away.

Walking. He was walking. Ambling almost. There was nothing hurried about his step in the least. We saw him reach into his pocket as he strolled past a line of parked cars. He stopped before one: a low, black sports car. Casually he put the keys in the door and began to open it.

"What . . . I mean, what . . ." said Tammany Bird.

"The hell?" I suggested.

"Come on, damn it," he said.

We let the fire door swing shut behind us. We started around the building to the front. Unlike Brandt, we were hurrying. It was something neither of us was very good at. Bird was such a huge man that the effort of carrying his weight made him breathless almost at once. As for me, I'd had it. My body had stood for enough abuse in the last couple of days.

Before we even came around the school, we were puffing in unison. I started coughing. Bird kept cursing and muttering "Come on" to his own legs. We headed for the patrol car. When we reached it, I leaned against it, trying to catch my breath. Bird unlocked it and let me in.

I fell into the passenger seat, dragging the door shut behind me. Bird got the car started. With a screech of tires, he pulled away from the curb.

"You all right?" he wheezed.

I tried to speak. I was seized with a fit of coughing. I felt the inhaled tar of a lifetime rising in my throat. I felt the blood rushing to my face. I leaned forward, hacking. Bird brought the cruiser around the corner.

"Eyeah," I gasped. "I'm fine."

The road ran straight. We sighted Brandt's sports car about three blocks ahead of us. It was cruising along at an even speed through a residential section. Its motion remained cool, unhurried.

"What the hell is he doing?" Bird said. His breath still whistled in his throat.

"I don't know."

"I mean, should I turn on the siren?"

"Yeah."

"Should I?"

"I don't know." I coughed.

"He ain't running."

"No."

"Let's see where he goes."

He went another block, then eased to a stop at the stop sign. His right-turn flasher blinked. As we stared after him, he went around the corner out of sight.

"I'll be jiggered," said Bird. He hit the gas. The cruiser spurted forward. I was thrown back against the seat. I grunted. Bird gasped. We shot ahead. We reached the corner where Brandt had turned. Another car was moving into the intersection from the left. We ploughed through the stop sign. We heard the blare of a horn, the scream of brakes. We missed a broadside by about a foot. Brandt had disappeared. We raced after him.

After about three blocks we found him again. He was two blocks ahead of us. He had sidled up to the curb in front of a white colonial home. He was getting out now: casually, slowly. He locked the car door. He strolled up the path to the house. We watched him. He opened the front door and went inside.

"What the hell? I mean, what the hell?" said Tammany Bird.

"Just let's nail him," I said.

Bird hit the gas again. The patrol car zipped through another stop sign. We screeched to a halt, skewed at an angle to the curb behind Brandt's neatly parked car.

We jumped out. We hustled up the walk. We stood before Dutch doors flanked by thin windows laced with copper cames. Bird rang the doorbell. It went dingdong. I peered through the windows. I saw the front hall and a flight of stairs.

We waited. There was no answer. Bird rang the doorbell again. It went dingdong again. I looked to my left and saw a large picture window. It hung above a patch of pachysandra planted up against the side of the house. I moved away from the door and began kicking through the pachysandra. I heard Bird whap the door with his palm.

"Open up," he shouted. "Open up, Brandt, it's Chief Bird."

I reached the window and peered in. I saw a living room, appointed with wooden, colonial chairs. Modest but stately. It was lit only by the light from outside. Beyond it I saw a long hall. It was completely dark. At the end of the hall was a room, lighted from within. It looked like a den. I saw a leather desk chair and part of a desk. Then I saw Brandt.

He was in the den. He moved into my vision from the left of the doorway. He was carrying a revolver.

"Bird, Bird, he's got a gun!" I shouted.

Reflexively the chief grabbed the door handle and tried to shove the door open. It wouldn't budge.

I saw Brandt sit down in the chair. He opened a drawer of his desk and brought something out of it. A little box. Bullets. He cracked open the revolver's cylinder. He fumbled with the box.

I kicked my way through the pachysandra, heading back to Bird. The chief was still trying to open the door.

"Shoot the goddamn lock off!" I cried.

He paused, faced me. "Wells," he said, "I'm the chief. I don't carry a weapon."

I threw myself at the door. Slammed against it with my shoulder. I grabbed my shoulder and screamed in pain.

"Bust the window," said Bird.

"You bust the window. Ow, God."

"Cut my goddamn hand off," Bird muttered. He stepped to the left. With a short, sharp blow, he hit one of the glass panes with the heel of his palm. The little pane cracked in half. The top half fell inward. Quickly the chief wriggled the bottom half free and tossed it into the pachysandra. He reached through the pane. I grabbed the door handle.

" 'Fi cut myself . . ." Bird muttered as he fumbled for the lock. ". . . take it out of your goddamn hide . . ."

"Hurry."

"You want to do this?"

"Would you hurry."

"I'm sixty-three goddamn years old . . . Got it."

I heard the latch shoot back. I pressed the handle. The door swung open. I went over the threshold running.

"Hey," Bird shouted. "He's got a gun, remember?"

But I was tearing through the living room, dodging the chairs. I raced into the darkened hallway. There was Brandt before me as I ran. I saw him snap the revolver shut. His face, though pale, was still calm. I was five steps from the door. If he wheeled and fired, I was a dead man.

He raised the revolver. But he did not turn. He placed the long barrel of the gun snugly under his right eyebrow.

I crossed the room's threshold. I leapt at him.

He pulled the trigger.

33

There have been a dozen moments in my life like that one. There have been too many. Gunshot moments that seem to spread across the fabric of time like an ink stain.

I felt my body in the air. I felt my hand wrapping itself around Brandt's wrist. Every atom of me seemed awake to the instant, and the instant seemed to last forever.

The gun went off. It wasn't very loud. Like every pistol shot I've ever heard, it sounded phony: like the rolls of caps I used to set off with a baseball bat when I was a kid. I had time to think about that as I flew toward Brandt, as I grabbed his wrist, as he fired. As I rolled across the desk, as I tumbled off and fell to the floor in what seemed like slow motion, I had time to imagine Brandt's blood and brains erupting above me, time to expect a rain of gore to come pouring down over me in the moment to come.

I hit the floor. Time suddenly sped up again. I felt the blow of the fall. I felt my breath knocked out of me. The room spun. I saw Brandt's face, twisted in horror. I saw Bird, frozen at the door.

Then the rain came. But it wasn't a rain of blood. It was a gentle, vaguely ridiculous snowfall of plaster and paint. The shot had blown a hole in the ceiling.

The gun had gone spinning out of Brandt's hand to land at Bird's feet. The chief stooped over heavily and picked it up.

Seated at his desk, the principal of the Grant Valley High School buried his face in his hands and sobbed.

"How many have there been?" said Bird.

Brandt sat hunched in a metal chair at a long table. The

chief sat across from him. I was leaning against the wall. We were in the station's conference room: a naked rectangle of a place, with only the table and chairs for furniture. There were no windows.

Brandt sat with his hands folded in his lap. His eyes were turned down to the table. He had the bare, dazed look some men get when they take off their glasses. His lips worked for a long time before any sound came out.

"Eight," he said hoarsely. The deep, sincere voice was gone. "Ten maybe." He knit his brows like he was trying to work it out. "I've been at the school ten years. Maybe ten."

Bird heaved an enormous sigh. "One a year," he said.

"I truly have tried to stop it," whispered Brandt. "I truly have." He looked up, first at Bird, then at me. He appealed to us. "They're just so beautiful."

"And young," said Bird.

Brandt's head fell. His lips pressed together. "I truly have tried. I knew no one would understand. I knew it would come out eventually, and then . . . Do you think . . . Do you think I'll have to go to jail?"

"Well, that depends." Bird rubbed his big face with his big hand. "There is the little matter of statutory rape. Are you positive you don't want an attorney?"

"Yes." I could barely hear him. He said it again. "Yes. What good would an attorney do me? I don't care what happens. Everything's over for me anyway. My career, I mean. Over. That's all that's ever really been important to me. My career. The kids . . ."

A moment passed in silence. Then Bird said, "Tell us about Nancy Scofield."

One corner of Brandt's mouth lifted in a miserable smile. "A sweet girl. A sweet, sweet girl. You don't know . . . You don't know the hell I've been through since she . . . Oh God, it's been so awful for me."

"Do tell," said Bird, under his breath.

"She was just . . . so lonely. An ugly-duckling type, didn't fit in anywhere, didn't realize her own . . . potential for . . . for sensuality."

Both Bird and I turned our faces from him.

"Oh, I know what you're thinking," said the principal,

looking up quickly. "You're thinking I'm a terrible man. But I'm not. Not really. I made her very happy for a while. It's just . . . she was just . . . too lonely. She started to care for me . . . too much, and I . . . I told her. I told her it was wrong, that it had to end, but she wouldn't listen. And when it was over . . ." He lifted his shoulders. "She just cried and cried."

"How long was that before she killed herself?" Bird asked him.

"About a week, a little more. It lasted through the summer. I didn't want it to. But she cared so much, I . . ."

It explained the transformation in Nancy's character. Her happiness through the summer. And the sudden plunge.

Now Bird shifted heavily in his chair, straightening. "Okay," he said softly. "Now tell us about Michelle."

Brandt blinked. "Michelle."

"Michelle Thayer."

Slowly he began to shake his head. "I never . . . Not with Michelle . . . no, I never . . ."

"But she knew about you and Nancy, didn't she?"

"No, I . . ."

"Nancy called her on the hotline and told her."

"The hotline? I didn't . . ."

"Mr. Brandt," Bird said. "You were willing to kill yourself to keep from facing a scandal."

"I . . . I don't know . . . I'd been waiting for it to happen so long . . . I . . ."

"What about Michelle? Were you willing to kill her too?"

Brandt's mouth did not drop open: it yawned open slowly. His eyes, too, widened in the long shock of the blow. Then he whispered, "Oh God. Oh God. Oh God."

"Where were you the night Michelle Thayer hanged herself?" asked Bird.

And Brandt laughed once suddenly. "Where? . . . Where was I? You sound like a television show."

"Not a television show, Mr. Brandt. Where were you?"

"I . . . I have no idea. Yes, I do. Wait. Yes, I do. I was at home. I got a phone call from her homeroom teacher, Mrs. Cotes. She called me. It was . . . it was early in the morning. Six or so. Before school started."

"What about that night?"

"I was at home. I was . . ."

"What?"

"I was drinking. Because of Nancy."

Bird and I looked at each other. "Anyone call you, visit you at home that night?" the chief asked.

"No, I . . . Yes, wait! Yes! Coach Wily did. Bob Wily, the gym coach. He called me. To talk to me about a football player . . . he'd been having trouble in school . . . he wanted to tell me that they'd talked. I can't remember the student's name, but he called me. I swear."

Their voices droned on. Bird asked more questions, Brandt fumbled through his shock for the answers. But now, as I leaned against the wall, I was no longer listening. My mind drifted away.

The thing of it was: I believed him. Bird would check it out with the gym coach, sure, but I was already certain that Brandt was telling the truth. He was a creep, one way and another, our principal. He was the kind of walking scar a teenaged girl could carry with her for a long, long time. But I knew the minute he heard Michelle's name that he hadn't killed her.

And then, in the next minute, I thought I knew who had.

It didn't come to me all at once. It more or less rose up out of my undermind until I was just sort of standing in the middle of it, looking it in the face. It was as if I'd been collecting personalities for the past few days—the Scofields, the Summers, Brandt, all the people I'd talked to. That I'd stored them all somewhere carelessly, in a jumble. And now, as I stood there with Bird and Brandt going at each other, now they sorted themselves out for me and I saw all of them for what they were.

Bird glanced up at me as I excused myself from the room. A wan glance. Annoyed. It was me who'd gotten him into this in the first place, stuck him with a scandal he didn't need. And here I was ducking out at the first opportunity. But it was moving toward afternoon, and I had plenty to do.

I wanted to be sure this time. I wanted to be absolutely sure.

34

The station house occupied the first floor of the county hall. Most of the files and records were on the fourth. An ancient elevator the size of a warehouse took me up there. It let me off in a huge expanse, almost glaring with the light of its huge windows. Gleaming in that light under pale fluorescents were dozens of battered, gunmetal filing cabinets. A few ancients sat on high stools here and there, files open on the tables before them. Their frail, liver-spotted hands listlessly turned the pages. The place stank of dust and the unexamined facts.

I went to the central desk. An old woman there gave me some forms. I filled them out. She gave me some files. She carried my forms away slowly. I guess they also went into a file somewhere. Everything went into the files.

I took my files to a table. I sat on a high stool. I began to read. The afternoon hours passed into evening. The seconds and the minutes and the hours. They went on and on like an old man's yarn. I kept the files before me. The pages of them fluttered by beneath my hands.

At four-thirty on the dot the old lady at the central desk rang a little bell. As if by reflex, the other old people around me closed their files and carried them back to her. I followed suit. I wasn't finished, not completely. I could have gone on for another day, at least. But I had enough for what I wanted. I wanted to flush my killer out, and I had enough for that.

I debated for a moment whether to go right to Chief Bird. I decided to wait. In the first place, I was guessing and I knew it. After Brandt, I didn't have the guts to drag Bird on another wild-goose chase. I didn't think it would accomplish much. This one was smarter than Brandt. This one would ask for a lawyer, would make no confessions. This one, also, was after me. I was the one who could tap the rage and self-hatred that might bring out the truth. There would be time, I thought, to call Bird in if things got out of hand.

The long November dark had fallen by the time I headed for the Summers' place. The night was as cloudy as the day had been, and colder. I drove into the Grant Valley woods on unlighted roads. Only the big houses here and there behind the trees marked the way.

The ranch house itself looked warm and inviting. All its big windows were bright with yellow light. Alice Summers opened the door for me. I saw that little worried smile of hers fade from her pretty face.

"Why? . . . " she began, and then thought better of it. She knew her job. She turned over her shoulder and said, "Walter, would you come here please."

I waited. Then the tan and handsome face of the politician was before me—glowering at me, in fact, with its best expression of moral outrage.

"I don't think we have any more business with you, Mr. Wells," he announced.

"Think another time," I told him. He began to shut the door in my face. "Think about Capstandard." The door stopped closing. "Think about American Regions," I said, "and about United Metals. . . ." The door swung open. Summers looked pale beneath his tan, but he managed to keep his moral outrage in place. "May I come in?" I said.

Well, he didn't say no anyway. I went in. I walked into the broad living room where the trophies of Summer's manhood were displayed. Michael Summers was seated in a leather easy chair, sipping a soda. He smiled when he saw me and began to stand up. The smile died when he saw the look on his father's face. He sat down again.

Walter Summers went past me, and I went after him. He led me out of the room and down a short hallway. We passed into a small study, all studded leather and dark brown wood. Globes and pictures of hunting dogs. More musk, more trophies.

He sat behind his desk and gestured me to a chair.

"I won't be long," I said. "I'll stand."

Summers nodded once. "That's fine. State your case and get out."

"All right. My case is this: you're crooked. You're dirty. You're a bought man. The electric trains are coming to Grant Valley and there's big money to be made in land, and you're the one making it, and you're not making it clean. Capstandard and all those other companies, they're coming into the county and chewing it to pieces. And you hold the door for them, and they tip you as they go."

Summers's mouth had become a thin, white line. "Is that right?" he said.

"Yeah, as a matter of fact, it is. I knew the second I saw the Capstandard office park that it was going to pollute the swampland under it. But your engineering firm helped it get a clean environmental report. Then you make pretty speeches at the legislature about how you wouldn't cast a vote but it was A-OK with you. That's nice. It's smart. It's subtle. And I'll bet it's lucrative too."

Summers just stared at me.

"I spent some time at county hall today. I tracked down some of those other companies your firm has worked for. You were on the Zoning Board of Appeals when United Metals got a variance on the access road laws. If that place ever blows up, and it well might, there's no way a fire truck could get to it. You brought the board around, Mr. Summers, you were the deciding vote. Not as subtle, but I'll bet it was just as lucrative. And then there's American Regions—"

"What exactly are you waiting for, Mr. Wells?" Summers said. "A confession?"

The controlled tone of his voice unnerved me, but I tried to keep pace. "Go ahead. Humor me," I said.

"Your reputation around here isn't worth a thin dime. You print this garbage and it'll be lining bird cages before it's even read."

"I don't think the State Investigation Commission keeps birds," I said.

He smiled thinly. "Nice try, Mr. Wells," he said. "Nice bluff. But all my votes and reports are public record. I have nothing to hide."

"Nothing but the money."

He stood up. "Then when you find it," he said, "let me know."

I cursed silently. I made my last stand. "I will," I said. "Sooner or later, I will."

"Well then, you'd just better get busy right away then, hadn't you?"

Alice and Michael Summers were both sitting in the living room when I passed through again. This time neither of them smiled at all.

35

When I got back to my hotel room, I threw my coat down on the bed angrily. I went for the desk, for the bottle I kept there. I needed a drink bad. A drink and a cigarette. I poured one, lit the other. I thought about calling Bird but it seemed out of the question now.

As I sat down, I noticed the message light on my phone was blinking.

"What the hell do you want?" I asked it. I snapped up the phone and rang the desk.

"Oh, yes. Mr. Wells," said the night clerk. Her voice was cracked and harsh. She managed to sound arrogant and incompetent at the same time. For some reason, I hadn't really been a welcomed guest since the police hauled the dead dog out of the woods. "Yes, there was something for you. I wrote it down. Here it is. A woman named Sandra Burr."

"Chandler Burke. When'd she call?"

"Oh, not long ago. I don't remember exactly. Oh . . . here's another. She called twice, that's right."

"She leave a message? A number?" I said through my teeth.

"Uh, something . . . She says she's at a hot line."

"What about? . . . "

"And that it's urgent."

"Great. Anything else?"

"No. Oh. Well, I guess you could say so."

"Let's."

"Someone called a couple of times asking for you. But he wouldn't leave his name."

"A man?"

"Yes. At least, I think so. It was hard to tell."

"All right. Thanks," I said. I pressed down the plunger. I rang Chandler. I was surprised. No busy signal: a ring on the first try. She was there. "It must be a slow day for despair," I said.

"I've been keeping the lines open. I've got an emergency on my hands and I'm here by myself." I waited. "A boy named Chris Thomas is suicidal."

"What?"

"Then you do know him."

"Yeah, he sent me to you."

"Oh, I thought . . . Well, I didn't know. Anyway, that explains it. I haven't been able to keep him on the line. He says he has to talk to you. He says you're the only one who understands. He hasn't been able to find you all day, and he's in a real panic. He's talking about slashing his wrists."

"Oh man. Is he serious?"

"I'd say so, yes. I promised him I'd track you down. It was the only way I could hold him back. He's supposed to call again in half an hour." I heard the relief in her breath. "I wasn't sure I'd find you in time. I thought you'd call."

I let that pass. "Did anything happen? To Chris, I mean. To set him off."

"I don't know. I don't think so. Just a conversation he seems to have had with you. He said something like, you shouldn't have brought him back to reality. That it's worse than the nightmare."

"Oh swell." I hesitated. "Can you get him to call my hotel?" I asked her.

"He says he won't do it anymore. He says the receptionist was nasty to him. He says she'll listen in on the conversation if he calls. Frankly, I talked to her, too, and I tend to agree with him. I've called four times in the past hour or so and I've only gotten an answer twice. If there were some foul-up . . ." She paused. Softly, she said: "I hate to drag you out here, John. But he's on the very edge."

I'd already grabbed my coat.

36

My nerves were shot. Grant Valley had been bad for them. I longed for the peace and quiet of Manhattan. Or a night's sleep. Or anything but being under siege on hostile ground.

The drive to St. Andrew's didn't help much either. I kept seeing headlights appear and reappear in my rearview mirror. I thought about Death, pulling out of the mist, running me off the road. My nerves were shot. I shook my head. I kept my eyes forward. I lit cigarette after cigarette as I drove on.

The lights behind me were gone by the time I reached the church. There was only the dark. I parked the car beneath the crumbling shadow of the place. I got out and hurried over the gravel path to the door. Once again the door creaked when I opened it. I didn't laugh at the melodrama this time. This time I wasn't in the mood. I entered the blackness of the chapel. Even the stained-glass windows had faded to gray shapes tonight. I stood still, my heart beating heavily, waiting for my eyes to adjust so I could move forward.

There was a flash. "John!"

I spun toward the sound, my fist cocked. I saw Chandler standing by the curtain near the altar. She was holding a flashlight in her hand. She leveled it over the pews. I went toward her.

"We can't afford to light the upstairs yet. This is S.O.P. for arriving shifts."

I tried to make a laughing noise. Even I wasn't convinced.

Chandler played the flash over my face. "You look beat," she said.

"I'm too old to have an entire county gunning for me."

She reached up and kissed me. "I'm on your side," she said.

"Well, then we've got 'em outnumbered."

She led the way down the stairs to the little room that housed the hotline.

The place was empty, silent. Two of the three phones on the table were off the hook.

"You here alone?" I asked.

"Yes. It still happens more than I'd like."

She smiled at me. It was a thin, weary smile. I wanted to kiss it, but I didn't. I wanted to breathe in the scent of her, but I moved away. If I relaxed now, I would collapse. I wanted to collapse, but I said, "What do I need to know?"

Chandler spoke slowly, softly. "Just listen to what he says," she told me. "Try not to judge him. Don't tell him to cheer up, or that things aren't so bad. Things are bad. Let him tell you about it. Ask questions if he won't talk. Remember: he's in trouble, but he did make the call. He must want to live. Let him talk, help him find that out, help him look at his options, help him find his way."

"You make it sound easy."

"It's not. You've got a real chance of losing him."

The phone rang. I jumped a little. Chandler picked up. She spoke into the receiver almost tenderly. "Hello, may I help you?" She listened. "Chris, I'm glad you called back. He's right here. He wants to talk to you."

She handed me the phone.

For a moment I couldn't lift the thing to my ear. I stood there with the transmitter pressed to my chest in my shaking hand. It seemed to me in some way that I'd spent a long time waiting for this to happen. And now that it was here, I dreaded it. I closed my eyes and took a breath. Behind my eyelids it was there, it was all still there. My daughter, my Olivia, in the port-red death robe she never wore. The scaffold above her that never was. The trapdoor, the sound of the trapdoor, the finality of it. Still there. All of it. Still there.

I brought the handset to my ear quickly. "Chris. How's it going, pal?"

He tried to say my name. He couldn't. He was crying too hard. I let him cry. It went on for a minute, a minute and a half. I reached into my coat pocket for a cigarette. There were none left. I brought out the empty pack and crushed it.

"I can't . . ." said Chris. It was a painful sound. It hurt me.

"Where are you?" I asked him—but Chandler waved her hand at me, shook her head. "Try and tell me what's wrong."

Through the sobs, the words came out in a rush. "I don't know, I don't know. It's just like . . . there's too much of it, too much."

"All right. Too much what?"

"The dying," he said. He grew quieter. "The dying. The losing people. I can't stand it. My old man, my father, Michelle. I can't . . . What's the point of it anyway?" I didn't have the answer to that one. I just waited. "You know, before . . . before I talked to you . . . in the graveyard and all . . . it was like . . . there was Death, I could see him. There was Death in the woods. It was like, I was on some kind of mission or something like in the movies: to get him, to stop him. But that's not real, is it? It's just a man in a mask, right? You told me that. You can't stop death. Not really. It just keeps coming, and whenever you love somebody . . . Oh God, it hurts so bad, Mr. Wells. It hurts like fire."

"Yeah," I said. I sounded hoarse. "Yeah, it does."

"I loved her. You know? Michelle. She talked to me. I loved her. Why did she die? Can you tell me that? Why did she have to die?"

I opened my mouth, but nothing came out. My mind felt jammed up. I felt panic rising in my belly. I didn't have the answers. I was going to lose him.

"Can you tell me?" he repeated.

"No. No one can tell you that. Not in the way you mean."

I heard him take a trembling breath. He was still crying. "Well, then what the hell's the point, you know what I mean? I mean, everything everybody says is just a lie then, isn't it? I mean, all the speeches people make, and all the, all the ideas they come up with, and all the terrible things they do to each other. They're just scared, aren't they? Everybody. They're just all scared because they know it's all just, it's all just dying and dying."

"Maybe so," I said.

"All those people on TV, you know, smiling, and all the priests and the president and all the teachers and everybody. They're just smiling and saying stuff . . . 'cause they don't really know anything, do they?"

I held the phone in my left hand for a moment. I wiped my hand on my pant leg. I wiped my brow with my sleeve. I glanced up at Chandler. She was sitting on the edge of the desk, watching me closely. I saw pity in her eyes.

And then, over the phone line, from wherever he was, Chris Thomas cried out in anguish, "Do they? Do they?"

"No," I said. "You're right. They don't really know anything."

And then softly: "You either."

"Me either," I said. And I thought: maybe me most of all.

There was a long pause. When Chris spoke next, the tears were gone. In their place was a quiet certainty that chilled me. "I want to get it over with," he said. "I just want to die. I'm going into the woods tonight, into the caves where no one will find me. I'm going to cut my wrists, and then it won't hurt so much anymore. Because I can't stand it, Mr. Wells. I tried, I really did. But it's all real, you know. It's all real. And I can't stand it."

I wanted to talk. I wanted to say something. Anything. Everything. Instead I was silent. My eyes passed desperately over the jumble of newspaper stories covering the walls. The room was filled with my silence. And the silence was filled with the sound of a trapdoor.

"I'm going now," said Chris, still quiet, still certain. "I guess—I guess I just wanted to say good-bye because . . . because I know you hurt too. I know it."

I still could not answer him. I was paralyzed by a sense of failure. Why couldn't I do anything? Why couldn't I help him? They die so young, so young, and what do we have to offer them to keep them here? If I had been there, I thought in my confusion . . . If I had been there with her when she walked into the woods, when she climbed the scaffold in her port-wine robe, when she stood on the trapdoor—would I have been silent then as I was now? I was her father, for

God's sake. I should have been there. How, having failed her so terribly, could I presume to sell the world to Chris?

The silence stretched out. I could feel him on the other end of the line. He was holding on, still holding on, still hoping I would come up with something, anything, that would give him a reason to fight it out. I didn't have his life in my hands; only the next minute, the next hour, the next day. But if I could come through for him, that might be all he needed.

And I stood there, silent, thinking: I should have been there, Olivia. I should have been there.

"I guess I just wanted to say good-bye," Chris said again.

My eyes went desperately to Chandler. But she was not looking at me now. Her face was lifted to the ceiling. Her body was tense. Her head was cocked in an attitude of listening. Her eyes were wide in an expression, half puzzled and half afraid.

She moved to her desk. Grabbed a piece of paper and a pencil. She scribbled something.

"Chris," I said, just to say something. "Tell me more."

He didn't answer. For a second I thought he was gone. Then I heard him let his breath out, as if he'd made up his mind.

Chandler stepped across the room and handed me the piece of paper. On it she'd scribbled the words: "Someone just drove up to the church."

37

"Okay," Chris Thomas whispered sadly. "Good-bye, Mr. Wells."

On the syllable of my name, I heard him move the phone away from his lips. He was going to hang up.

I shouted, "Wait, Chris! Wait! There is something!"

I gripped the phone hard. I listened to dead air. I waited for the click and the tone.

"What?" said Chris Thomas.

I caught my breath. I was desperate. I had no idea what I was going to say. I took the pencil out of Chandler's hand. I wrote on the scrap of paper: "Cops. Now."

Chandler nodded and moved to one of the other phones.

"Chris," I said. "Are you still there?"

The pause seemed to last forever. In that pause I heard the sound of the church door creaking open upstairs. I glanced at the ceiling. I ran my fingers through my hair. My hair was wet with sweat.

"Yeah," said Chris, uncertain. "Yeah, I'm here."

"Then listen," I said. And as I spoke, something gave way in me, something that had been there for a long time. I felt it break like a dam at floodtide, and finally the words came. "Everything you say, I guess it's true," I told him. "Everybody's talking all the time, making pronouncements and everything. But nobody—nobody really knows much of anything in the end. The president and the movie stars and the, the music people you guys like. They're just as scared as you are. And me. Maybe . . . Maybe the thing is . . . maybe they're trying to convince themselves that there's a secret, that life is a fair deal that can be worked out. Maybe they think, you know, that if they handle things just right, get right with God or whatever, it'll all turn out okay." I shook my head. The room was blurring in front of me. Beside me I heard Chandler murmuring into the phone to the police. Above me I heard the church door swing shut with a thud.

But the words kept coming. They weren't my words, I realized now. They were my daughter's. They were the words she'd written to me in her last letter, the truth she'd learned but couldn't live by. They were her legacy, I guess. A legacy I'd never accepted. Now, though, I fought to speak clearly, to come to grips with it, to pass it on. "It isn't fair, buddy," I said. "It doesn't turn out okay. It isn't fair or unfair or nice or not nice. People live and they die and if there's a reason, it's more than I can tell you. It just is. It's just the way it is.

"I guess you have to play it that way, just for what it is, just for the fact that it is. You got to play it down the line, with all the dying and the pain of it, and the good-byes and the hurting inside. I mean the thing is, kid, you don't have to kill yourself to die. You can trust me on that. I'm an expert. If the hurt is bad enough, you can bury yourself alive. You can bury yourself a thousand ways. Believe me. I know most of them. But maybe, if you play it out, if you play it for all it's worth . . . maybe it isn't fair or unfair or anything like that . . . but maybe it's sweet, you know? Maybe it's sweet as wine. Maybe it's just worth it. Maybe it just is."

I stopped. I wiped my face with my hand. I couldn't talk anymore. Chandler had hung up her phone and sat beside me, watching me closely.

I heard Chris Thomas start to cry again. I heard him whisper: "I don't want to die, Mr. Wells. I want to live, man, I don't want to die."

Then I heard a footstep sound in the chapel above.

I took the phone away from my ear and handed it to Chandler. She waved her hand and shook her head, but I pressed it on her. She put her hand over the transmitter.

"You can't," she hissed. "We'll lose him."

I smiled a little. "I have to. I have nothing else to say."

I left her there. I moved to the door, opened it. I walked across the dark hall to the stair and felt for the banister.

I heard another footstep and another, moving tentatively among the pews.

Death was up there.

I went after him.

38

Long climb, up those stairs. There was no way to do it quietly, with the wooden boards complaining beneath my feet. There was no way to do it quickly. By the time I reached the landing, I figured my old friend in the skull mask knew where I was. But I knew that the police were on their way. It was all just a question of time.

I crested the stairs. I moved down the dark hallway. I pushed aside the curtain, and heard Death's footstep stop as I stepped into the blackness of the decaying chapel. He was somewhere in the center of the room, navigating his way slowly through the pews, looking for me. I squinted. I couldn't make him out. I moved away from the sound of him.

Trying not to smash into anything, I slowly went toward the altar. I didn't want the gray light from the stained-glass windows to give me away. My foot touched the altar step. I rose onto it. I kept moving. I figured I was standing directly in front of him now, that he was down the central aisle about twenty steps away.

From far to my right, then, came a low, animal growl: "Wells."

I turned swiftly, surprised by his location. As I turned, the clouds must have parted outside, the moon must have appeared. Suddenly the scarlet angel of the last trump was gleaming on the right wall. And branded into the lower folds of the angel's robe was the silhouette of Death's head.

"I can't say I'm surprised to see you in church, Michael," I said. "I know you're a religious man. At least I know you worship your father."

The angel vanished. The silhouette was gone. The clouds must have covered the moon.

Having spoken, I backpedaled rapidly, hoping he'd lose me again. I had to keep this going until I heard the sirens sound.

I was now under the altarpiece: a huge wood carving, askew, in disrepair. I felt the grim and twisted faces of the saints hanging over my shoulder. Staring down at me as if already prepared to mourn.

"Wells."

For a second, I couldn't place the sound of him in the dark. He'd moved away from the wall. Toward the center aisle again, I thought, and forward, closer to me.

"I guess it's tough when the gods fall down," I said, continuing to move. "How long have you known that your old man was crooked?"

He bumped into a pew. I heard it scrape against the floor. I thought I made out his half shadow on a wooden post near the room's center, but it was gone before I was sure.

I moved to the left, came slowly down the altar stairs again.

"You were an impressive keeper of the flame, Mike," I said. "You had me going a long time. That first time I met you, I was all ready to write about your father, about how he moved your brother to suicide. And you turned me around. Did it again at the board meeting . . . turned my attention from your dad's Capstandard speech. . . ."

Michael Summers growled inarticulately this time: the sound of pure rage. But it was too close a sound. Like me, he was on the altar stairs, though across the room. I stepped down to the floor and moved away from him, toward the wall to the left.

"But your brother, now . . . Fred . . . he wasn't a true believer like you, was he? When he found out that he'd spent his life trying to live up to the image of a crook, he lost his faith. He called the suicide hotline, talked to Michelle, told her everything. He told you that day out by the pond, the day he blew his brains out. I wonder what you said to him out there to make sure he punished himself for falling away from the great god Walter Summers. . . ."

"Wells!"

It was a scream this time, and I lost it completely in its own echoes. As I moved beneath the dull, faceless windows on the wall, I had no idea where he was.

"And then you went after Michelle," I said, as coolly as I could. "You made it just another teen suicide. Well, hell, it wasn't really murder, was it? You're Walter Summers's angel of death, aren't you? Your old man, he could've withstood the scandal, but not you . . . it would've made you face up to what he was . . . to the kind of man—"

And then I made a mistake. I stopped. In the distance, though I couldn't be sure, I thought I heard the scream of an oncoming siren. So I stopped, and I listened.

And in the deep, hollow groan of an opening coffin, I heard him say, "Wells." And he was right beside me.

I spun. Outside, the moon came out. St. Andrew's agonized face hung from the crucifix on the window above me. I saw it at the same moment I saw the skull of death rise out of the darkness, as I saw his jagged dagger flash up and into the air above my head. And then the knife came plunging down at me.

I raised my hands, crossed at the wrists. His forearm was caught in the crux. It pushed down. The edge of the knife slit my brow and blood splashed over the right side of my face.

I swung his captive arm to the side, hurling him away from me. He flew into the wall. But before I could move, he recovered. He rushed at me. For a terrifying instant I lost him in the dark between us.

Then all at once my vision was filled with the sight of the skull. I jabbed wildly at the death's head before me, striking with the stiffened fingers of my hand. Michael let out a high-pitched scream as my fingertips dug into his eye. I felt the whisper of the blade pass by my left side. Then he was reeling away from me.

I was sure I heard the sirens now. They were racing over the road beneath the hill, heading for the driveway that would lead them up here.

Michael heard it too. He had fallen to one knee. He was gripping the edge of a pew. But now he lifted his head to the sound. He clambered to his feet. He tore the mask from his head. And with a single glance at me, bounded for the door.

I didn't go after him. I couldn't have if I'd wanted to. I was just too beat. The flow of blood from my head had already slowed, but my left eye was glued shut with it. I was wheezing. My legs felt weak.

So I stood there, slumped and aching. And in another second or so the church door squeaked open. And there was Michael Summers, his arms flung wide, his head flung back, his mouth opened, and his wild voice baying his despair . . . framed in a frozen instant by the red fire of the police flashers as they came screaming up the hill.

I turned away. I pulled myself to my feet. I stumbled to the hallway, to the stairs.

"Chris," I mumbled to myself. "Chris . . . left him . . . God, not again . . . not again."

I went down, clutching the banister with one hand, trying to wipe the blood off my face with the other. I reached the bottom. I staggered toward the closed door of the hotline phone room.

I listened for Chandler's voice. I didn't hear it. I knew before I opened the door that she'd lost him: that I'd lost him, and she'd listened to him go.

My hand found the knob and turned it. In my mind, I heard that other door, the trapdoor, open once again.

I stepped in and saw Chandler. She was seated where I'd left her on the edge of the desk. The phone was still clutched in her hand, held to her ear. A single tear was rolling down her cheek, but her voice was warm and calm.

"It's all right, Chris," she kept saying, over and over. "It's all right now. It's going to be all right."

39

Good story. A murder hidden in a spate of teen suicides. It was a damn good story, and it was all mine. STAR ACE CRACKS KILLING. Cambridge went nuts with it. Even I couldn't blame him. We had it a day before the pack, and they were still calling us for interviews two days later. It was damn good stuff.

I finished most of the work on the thing. I tracked down the garage where Michael Summers kept his secret car. I found the place that sold the death mask, and Cambridge ordered me to do an entire feature on it. I even got an exclusive interview with Alice Summers the day after she left her husband, swearing she'd file for divorce.

The peak of it came about four weeks after the arrest. That was when the psychiatrists trooped into the county courthouse to tell the judge that Michael Summers wasn't fit to stand trial. Behind that perfectly controlled exterior, the judge was told, the boy was crazier than hell. Michael's confession, presented in open court, seemed to clinch it. He sat in the witness stand, staring blindly into space, reciting his crimes in a monotone: How he'd seduced Michelle into the woods. How he'd strangled her with the rope. How he'd strung up the body. He seemed to think it had happened to someone else. That, too, was good stuff.

Taken all in all, the testimony painted a picture of a young man obsessed with his father. In fact, it seemed Walter Summers had been an obsession for both his sons. He was larger than life to them. He held sway over their imaginations. And when they discovered he was corrupt, it had shattered their worlds. To Michael, who had a cool, sophisticated mind, the discovery came slowly, over the years. And over the years, he made adjustments to accommodate the information. Slowly, step-by-step, he adjusted himself right over the edge. Fred was luckier in a way. He was more of an innocent. He found out the truth about his dad in the course of one overheard phone conversation. He seemed, somehow, to feel responsible for what Walter was. He seemed to blame himself. Maybe that was the key to it: the difference in the personalities of the two brothers. Both Fred and Michael were willing to commit murder to protect their father—or to protect themselves from their sense of betrayal, their feelings of rage. But Fred murdered himself, while Michael murdered Michelle Thayer.

Michael had learned to wear a mask—but it was not the mask of Death. It was that smiling mask of maturity and self-possession, the mask of the controlled young man of the world. Death—Death, the avenger—that was the real Michael, all right, the only Michael who existed inside his head. So, when he was done with Michelle, when he knew he had evaded the law, he found himself at loose ends. What's an avenger, after all, without a victim? Then, luckily for him, I showed up.

I became his reason for being: the one, so he thought, who would turn up the truth about Michelle and, through Michelle, about Walter Summers. Michael was after me from the start. Virtually every action he took was designed both to get rid of me and to confess to me. The hanging dog was not only a threat, but a confession as well. The same with his ghostly appearance at Janet Thayer's house. When I found Chandler, when I started moving in on the truth, he knew he had to act. But even then—when he tried to kill me on the road, when he planned to lie in wait for me in my hotel room—he was pleading guilty. If he'd kept to himself, I might never have found him.

But he didn't. When I realized—by elimination more than anything—that Michelle had been killed to protect Walter Summers, I knew it wasn't Summers who'd done it, but his son. The old man wasn't afraid of me, he'd taken no special pains to cover up or avoid me. He felt pretty sure that he'd covered his tracks. It was Michael who was always there to protect his father's reputation. And I guessed that if I confronted the father, the son would show his hand. When Michael didn't react immediately, I thought I'd blown it. But he had more patience than I did.

Anyway, like I said, the confession was the high point of the story. After that, the whole thing faded away. A single murder, far from the city, over a month old. Even I was tired of it. Even Cambridge was ready to be pried loose. We let it fall to the metro section, and it was gone completely within the week.

But Cambridge had had his first warm blast of praise from the people upstairs, and his good feelings toward me continued to turn my stomach for months afterward. I'd cemented his position in the organization, God help me. He kept calling me "old friend," and "Wellsy." He was a regular guy, Cambridge was.

After a while I took a couple of days off. Chandler Burke came down from the county and stayed with me. We had a lot to talk about, twenty years worth. We didn't talk about it. We went to bed and made love, and then kept making love to one another again and again. It felt good. It felt like living.

She was still with me on Sunday, the day before I went back to work. The next day I was scheduled to pick up the Dellacroce trial. The key witnesses were still to come. I was looking forward to it.

That evening, I remember, Chandler was in the kitchen, making coffee. The plan was to go out to dinner: We were trying to get our bodies accustomed to being vertical again.

I was standing at the window with a cigarette in my hand, staring down at the movie marquee on Eighty-sixth street. The room was unlit around me. The bright white light of the marquee made me squint. It made my eyes water. My eyes were watering anyway. The marquee blurred.

Chandler came in and put the coffee mugs on my desk. She glanced at me, but didn't say anything. She came and stood next to me, looking out at the marquee.

After a while she just said: "How is it?"

I swallowed hard. "It's better," I said. "It's better."

"It'll get better," she whispered.

"Yeah. Yeah, sure it will."

She moved closer to me. The side of her touched me in the evening dark.

"Yeah," I said. I nodded. I kept nodding for a long time as the marquee blurred and shifted outside the window. The smoke from my cigarette drifted up before my eyes in a wavering line.

"My God," I said then. I put my arm around Chandler's shoulder. I shook my head. "My God, but I loved her."

ABOUT THE AUTHOR

Keith Peterson is a radio and newspaper journalist who lives in New York City. He's currently at work on the second book in the John Wells series. Under a pseudonym, he is an Edgar award winning author.

Kinsey Millhone is . . .

"The best new private eye."   —The Detroit News

"A tough-cookie with a soft center."   —Newsweek

"A stand-out specimen of the new female operatives."
                                        —Philadelphia Inquirer

Sue Grafton is . . .

The Shamus and Anthony Award winning creator of Kinsey
Millhone and quite simply one of the hottest new mystery
writers around.

Bantam is . . .

The proud publisher of Sue Grafton's Kinsey Millhone
mysteries:

    ☐ 26563 "A" IS FOR ALIBI $3.50
    ☐ 26061 "B" IS FOR BURGLAR $3.50
    ☐ 26468 "C" IS FOR CORPSE $3.50